BOOZEHOUNDS AND BALL DROPS

MYSTIC'S END MYSTERIES BOOK 6

LEANNE LEEDS

BADCHEN PUBLISHING

Boozehounds and Ball Drops
Published by Badchen Publishing
4500 Williams Dr., Suite 212-269
Georgetown, TX 78633 USA

For permissions contact: info@badchenpublishing.com

BOOZEHOUNDS AND BALL DROPS

ONE

W hen I moved to Mystic's End, I was looking for answers about where I came from, sure. And yes, maybe I wasn't looking for them that fast, but I *was* looking. I was also looking for peace, a place to belong. A small town I could run my art shop in, with locals I could teach, tourists I could sell original canvases to, a community I could build around art and beauty, around creativity.

But mostly peace. Peace and quiet.

I sat in the corner, watching the chaos swirl through my quaint little art shop.

Gabe and Ollie were precariously balancing a large whiteboard above their heads as the two picked their way through the shoppers who were gazing at the art on display. Claire leaned away from the men while she spoke to a customer about preserving an acrylic painting they had just purchased for a holiday gift. I could hear another woman shouting questions about framing options for a blue and green landscape Azalea had done. Behind the counter, I spotted Gideon and Petey chuffing and leaning into one another at her feet.

My art studio was finally filled with people after months of me struggling to make a go of it.

And yet...all I wanted was some peace and quiet.

"Excuse me. Excuse me, Miss? Are you the psychic artist?" I looked up from my seat on the floor behind the counter to find a well-dressed middle-aged woman leaning and pointing. She had thrust her substantial body so far forward I was concerned she would topple over. "I want a reading. Is this where I get a reading?" She waved a fistful of cash at me. "I want that special reading thing you do."

"Ma'am, you'll have to back up," Claire warned, hurrying over. "You can't lean on the counter like that. The glass isn't strong enough to support you."

"Are you calling me fat?" the heavy woman snapped.

"Of course not, ma'am," Claire responded, her eyes wide. "The counters are simply not supportive of anyone leaning on them that way."

"Well, how was I *supposed* to get her attention when she's hiding behind the counter on the floor? Throw pottery at her?"

"It's fine, Claire," I told my new assistant as I scrambled up off the floor. "I can take care of it."

"Are you sure?" Claire asked, her eyebrow raised. "You're looking a little peaked."

"Don't tell her *that*, Claire," Bella Grayson, recently deceased, told her ex-girlfriend. Claire's eyes unfocused as the app *Ghosts, Ghosts Everywhere* tried to translate the words spoken by the incorporeal Bella. While I could see and hear ghosts, my human friends needed their cell phones to talk to the great beyond. Claire had taken to wearing a small bluetooth bud hidden in her ear so she and Bella could speak to one another.

"I'm fine." As I nodded and turned to the customer, Ollie and Gabe accidentally whacked me in the back with the whiteboard they were moving. I turned and glared.

"You okay?" Ollie asked, mortified. I nodded.

"Have I mentioned today how much I appreciate you letting me rent an office in your shop, Fortuna?" Gabe asked, reddening slightly.

Gabe also spent most days with an earbud in his ear so he could hear his recently deceased grandmother, Miss Bessie. If she had something to say.

And Miss Bessie always had something to say.

"If you appreciate it so much, get the board out from her showroom floor, Gabriel!" Miss Bessie called from the back. Gabe's eyes unfocused, he reddened further, and he nodded. "It's the holiday season, let her make some money!"

"Miss? Oh, Miss?" The customer who wanted a reading shoved the money close to my face. So close, the distinct smell of cash blocked out the smell of paint thinner for a moment. "My reading! I came all this way just for a reading! Well, and to gamble this weekend at the casino and see a show," she added as she batted long, fake eyelashes at me. "But mostly for the reading!"

"If you'll follow me?" I gestured for her to come around the counter, and we followed Ollie and Gabe down a narrow hallway.

The narrow hallway had once been my muse room—a peacefully gentle room for meditation, relaxation, and contemplation. Now, the corridor lead to the back art studio where I taught art classes, bordered by two freshly constructed walls. One door on the right lead to Gabriel's new private detective office. To the left, my own "office"—a mini-muse room a third the size of what it used to be.

It was now where I took customers who wanted a psychic reading from the famous Mystic's End mystic.

* * *

"Just put the money in that jar," I told the woman after I closed the door, the hustle and bustle of my full shop quieting down. Gabe did do a great job with the walls and doors. He put sound-dampening material in each partition and fixed the entrances with solid-core doors to give both of us rooms we could talk openly in without fear of being overheard.

Within seconds, Gideon slipped in through the doggie door (which he insisted we put in for him) and made a beeline for his cushion in the corner of the room. With a few circles and a sigh, he flopped down and closed his eyes.

"Don't you want to count it?" she asked, astonished.

"Nope. I'm sure you'll give what you think the service is worth, and the money all goes to the greyhounds, anyway, ma'am. So if you decide to cheat me, you're really cheating the work greyhound rescues do." I told her with a shrug.

"Have you heard how this works?" I grabbed a small canvas and placed it on an easel.

"No, I just read about you in the paper. Do you read my palm or tea leaves or something?"

"The way this works is I will close my eyes," I said, arranging the paints on the stand beside me. "Once I have a clear picture of what I think you need to know, I will paint it."

"With your eyes closed?" she asked, her face sporting a look of astonishment.

I nodded. "I'm going to reproduce the vision in my mind on the canvas, and once it's done, it will be up to you to interpret why it was shown to you and what it means. Do you understand?"

The woman nodded slowly. "I think so. Don't you want to know my name?"

"No, ma'am," I told her. "I don't need to know anything about you. That way, there's no question that whatever I get is just from my own insight. Are you ready?"

As my psychic ability became more widely known—because my fake psychic vision was writ large in a photo on the front page of the town newspaper—I'd grown frustrated at the people showing up for readings. Before the story that I'd solved Bella Grayson's murder via vision, there had been a trickle. That publicity turned it into a deluge.

And folks seeking psychic guidance could be...wearying.

Exhausting.

Annoying.

There was always a contingent that just demanded that I tell them what to do. I grew tired of it and borrowed this method of communication from Gideon, my greyhound. To talk to me, he sent me images, and I had to figure them out. So, that's how I did readings now. I figured if I could do it with my dog, they could do it with me.

Oh, people still saw what they wanted to see, but at least I got to paint more.

"Now, clear your mind, and think about what it is you want to know," I told her as I turned toward the canvas and closed my eyes. The rich woman wanted to know if she would win a jackpot gambling at the casino this weekend. It was a good thing my eyes were closed. She couldn't see me roll them.

My hand flew over the canvas, quickly following the image in my mind's eyes. Within four minutes, I opened them to find a painting of the woman sitting, happily, at a slot machine. I had simply reproduced the memory of the enjoyment she had the last time she went, the joy the woman felt she was looking for once again. Whether she realized it or not, it's what she really wanted. To have fun.

When I turned the canvas toward her, she gasped. "That's amazing! How did you know?"

"I just did," I started, but then paused. The wall outside my office/reading parlor vibrated as something crashed against it. "If you like, we can ship the painting to you once it's dry. You just need to pay Claire for the canvas at the register and give her the shipping address. There's no specific charge for the painting part itself; that's part of the reading."

"Oh, I don't care about the painting," she scoffed, waving away the offer. "Thank you so much!"

"Of course." I nodded, and she swept out the door, convinced that she would add to her pile of dragon's gold this holiday weekend. Once the door slammed behind her, I waved my hand in front of the canvas. The paint quickly made its way back onto the palette and then marched its way back into the tube—no reason to waste resources.

"You're getting better at that," Miss Bessie said, her head shoved halfway through the wall.

"It keeps the costs down." I shrugged. "What was that loud bang?"

"Gabriel tripped. I think they're almost done with moving things in, though I still don't understand why they couldn't go through the back."

"Private birthday party," I told her. I glanced at the cash in the jar. Noting that the reading money was adding up, I realized I probably needed to make a bank run and deposit it in PeeGrrr's account after Thanksgiving. "Azalea should be wrapping it up now, but I didn't want to interrupt them when they paid for space. I know Gabe wanted to be done before Thanksgiving tomorrow."

"Who cares when Gabe wants to be done?" Miss Bessie floated into the room and crossed her arms. "You're doing him a favor by letting him open up his detective agency in your little art shop, anyway. He should do things on your timeline, not his."

A gentle knock at the door interrupted the old woman's rant, and Gabe slipped in. "I assume my grandmother's in here," he told me, glancing around. "You may want to let her know that the app is cluing me in on what she's saying. Well," he frowned. "More or less."

"I can hear you, sweet cheeks," Miss Bessie snapped. A moment later, Gabe winced.

"I *really* am sorry about the mess. This was the only day Ollie had off, and the only day we could get the moving truck. Well, besides Thanksgiving itself, and you already nixed that. We're almost done, though. Just a wing chair left to bring in, and then we're all settled."

"I didn't nix it, I just feel like we deserve an *actual* Thanksgiving holiday." I grabbed a sweater from my smock rack and slipped my arms into it. It was a little chillier than I expected—probably due to Gabe and Ollie going in and out of the front door, letting all the heat out. It was odd, too, because I didn't get cold often. I was the weird chick who could go for a walk in winter in a t-shirt. Miss Bessie suspected it was due to magical energy, that real witches had so much it kept us warm.

"You okay?" Gabe asked, concerned.

"Yeah, just a little chilly, that's all."

"So who's coming tomorrow?"

"Pepper, you, Claire, Liz. That's it. I invited Ollie, but he's going to his dad's. He said he'd try and stop by later, but that's it. Well, obviously, all the ghosts will be here."

"How are you going to cook Thanksgiving dinner for five people in a toaster oven?" he asked, surprised. One of the first things Gabe had commented on when he met me—well, after asking how a dead body wound up in my wall—was why I didn't finish out the kitchen. With a hot plate and a convection toaster oven, I thought I *had*.

"I ordered it from the diner," I answered sheepishly.

Gabe shook his head. "At some point, we're going to get a range, Fortuna. Especially if I'm going to be working here." He tilted his head. "Tell you what, let me contribute a range to the kitchen. It's the least I can do."

I shook my head. "No. That's not necessary. You already put all this work into—"

"Destroying your muse room and replacing it with two offices?" he asked impishly. His face grew serious. "You didn't invite Martin or Jeeves to dinner tomorrow night?"

"No."

I guess the look on my face clarified I didn't want to talk about it, because he nodded and said nothing more.

* * *

"I really miss turkey," Spike, my first spectral roommate, complained while he watched me hook up a multi-device bluetooth speaker. "And gravy. Oh, man, gravy is the best. I wish I could eat again," he sighed.

"You can fly, boy. Don't be ungrateful," Miss Bessie told the punky young man. "If you had any idea what it was like to get old, you wouldn't be complaining about your untimely youthful demise at all."

"I've never met someone so happy about being dead," Spike told her glumly.

"You've never met anyone dead other than Bella and me. Oh, and that mailman that got stuck in the rock," Miss Bessie ticked off on her fingers. "Let me tell you something. You live with bursitis, arthritis, GERD—"

"How long do you have to be dead before you stop complaining about the old lady diseases you don't have anymore?"

Miss Bessie fumed. "You watch your tone, youngster."

"I've been dead a lot longer than *you*, you know—"

As the two ghosts bickered, I stared at the fancy bluetooth speaker I'd purchased just so all the phones could carry the spectrally relevant observations of the spirits to everyone attending Thanksgiving. I had hoped they would feel like they were a part of the festivities—even if they could have no turkey.

Now, I scanned to make sure there was a mute button.

My cell phone rang, and I hurried away from the apparition octagon to grab it.

"Hello?"

"Fortuna, it's Jeeves," Martin's bodyguard said in his low, smooth voice.

Martin Salvi was the wealthiest man in town and the secret son of Marty Salvatore (aka the Dreamboat Don, aka the head of the Dastardly Crime Family). Well, *not that* much of a secret. It seemed like everyone knew Martin wasn't someone to be trifled with, but if they knew why, they never said it out loud.

Jeeves was Martin's vampiric bodyguard. The Dastardly Crime Family had risen to prominence by using a stable of paranormal folks—witches and vampires—to guard and enforce their dominance. Martin said they were employees and chose their life freely. I saw them as no better than indentured servants, indebted to the Salvatores for powerful magic or, in Jeeves's case, that he was a vampire at all.

"What do you want?" I asked coldly.

"I wanted to wish you a happy Thanksgiving," Jeeves said warmly, ignoring my tone. "I also wanted to ask you to refrain from working any magic until after the new year. If you wouldn't mind."

I frowned. Jeeves and Martin had been haranguing me to move faster on the magical mystery we were trying to solve—the location of the witch bottles of the Delphi Coven and their descendants. "Why the sudden about-face?" I asked him.

"Martin's father, Marty Salvatore, is in town for the holidays," Jeeves explained. "We are concerned that some of the witches he brought with him would be able to sense your magic, and we'd like to keep you...off his radar for the time being. Is that something you think you could do?"

I knew little about Martin's father, or his harem of witches. For a moment, I felt like reading Jeeves the riot act. I wanted to ask him who he thought he was, asking me to hide who I was just because Martin's mafioso father visited. Then I swallowed my arguments down.

It wouldn't be easy, but I could. And Jeeves was probably right—he was only in town a month, right? Why complicate the situation if I didn't need to? "Why are you calling now at the last minute?" I asked curiously.

"We did not know that he would be arriving until he did so, Fortuna. I apologize for the late notice, but I called you as soon as I was able." I could sense nothing from the vampire, but there was something in his voice that worried me. "Little magics should be fine. But no huge magical workings, and perhaps staying off the cauldron"—a magical communication and teleportation device —"would be best."

Martin's father, the mafia boss, arriving with no warning? "Sure, I can try," I told him. Then, lowering my voice, I asked, "Jeeves, is everything okay?"

"Well, Don Salvatore has just put Jerome in charge of the track for this week so he can spend some time with Martin. I suppose we shall soon know one way or another, won't we?" he answered without answering. And then he hung up.

TWO

I stirred, stretching my arms above my head. Gideon made odd little noises of greeting. "Hey there, buddy," I told him sleepily, rolling over to cuddle him for a moment before the busy day started. My first Thanksgiving in Mystic's End. I smiled to myself thinking about it. Who would have predicted I'd have such a full house of people before the end of my first year? Not me, that's for sure. I sighed as the smell of turkey cooking hit my nose—

—and then sat up in bed like a shot.

How did I smell turkey cooking?

I didn't have an oven.

I jumped out of bed, pulled my bathrobe around me, tied it tightly and hurriedly descended the stairs to the second floor—to find Gabe, his back to me, stirring something in a pot. On top of a *range*. Pepper stood beside him, pounding on something that might have been bread dough. Or pasta. Or clay.

I *did* mention I don't really cook, right?

"Morning, lazy bones! Happy Thanksgiving!" Pepper Stanford (full-time puff-piece writer, and aspiring investigative reporter) called cheerfully. "What do you think of your new range?"

"*Why* do I have a new range?" I asked, staring at the black and silver monstrosity. "How do I have a new range? That thing is huge."

"This is Miss Bessie's old BlueStar," Gabe said. "It's a much better range than mine, but it's a little big for my kitchen. I'd always wanted to redo it—my kitchen, I mean—so I could fit this thing, but just never got around to it. It was sitting in storage, so we moved it up here."

"How on earth did you get it up here without waking me?" I asked, stunned. The appliance was colossal and looked heavy. "Is that whole thing stainless steel?"

"It is," Miss Bessie told me as she floated in. "And you better take care of it. My husband worked hard to get me that range. It was probably my most prized possession, and I was not thrilled with the home when they wouldn't let me put it in my bedroom." The *Ghosts, Ghosts Everywhere* app piped an approximation of what Miss Bessie said through the speaker and into the room.

"Well, that's cool. We can all hear her," Pepper smiled, impressed. "Morning, Miss Bessie!"

Miss Bessie did not return her greeting. Instead, she eyed Pepper's work and said, "You're over-kneading that dough, Pepper. Those rolls are going to be as tightly wound as you."

Pepper stuck her tongue out, but stopped kneading and let the dough rest. Turning to me, she quipped, "That speaker has a volume, right?"

"And a mute button." Miss Bessie rolled her eyes at me. "I still don't get how on earth you got all this up here while I was asleep."

"Ollie and I got it up here," Gabe shrugged. "It wasn't hard."

"Of course it wasn't hard." Pepper leaned back and met my eyes. "They called Jeeves and asked if he could tiptoe it up the stairs for you. That vampire could lift an elephant with one hand tied behind his back."

"Jeeves is here?" I asked, looking around. My hand flew to my bra (which I now slept in) to make sure Samson's blocking stone was still against my skin. The vampire's telepathy was powerful, and the gem was the only thing that kept my thoughts protected.

She shook her head no and poured a cup of coffee. "He had to go back to Martin's. He was in a real hurry, too. He seemed distracted, which, for Jeeves, was a little weird."

"Martin's father's in town. Showed up unexpectedly." I accepted the cup of coffee from Pepper and sipped it. "When he called me about it last night, he seemed a little concerned. Asked me not to work magic while Marty Salvatore was in town, too." I frowned. "Sounds like he brought a witch brigade with him or something."

Pepper nodded and then glanced at the clock. "Shoot, the parade is on!" Pepper jumped and ran for the remote. "I didn't realize it was so late."

"Late?" I asked, yawning again. "It's nine in the morning."

"On Thanksgiving!" Pepper told me as cheerful announcers suddenly boomed through my television. She squealed like a child and clapped her hands, her eyes huge as she took in a float on TV. "It's the holidays, Fortuna! How can you not be excited about the holidays?"

I held up my mug. "I have about three quarters to go before I can be excited about anything."

"Well, drink up, then!" she laughed and waved at me. "It's happy season!"

I stared slack-jawed at my sarcastic, suspicious,

conspiracy-theory minded best friend who squealed and jumped and sang along to a Broadway show tune blasting at a volume I never realized my television could reach. "Did Pepper hit her head?" I asked Gabe.

He laughed. "You know how she's always suspicious, on the go, overly concerned with things? Too serious, overly studious, all that?" I nodded. "Every year, she takes a break from that. From Thanksgiving to New Year's, you get to see a side of Pepper's personality that's not very visible the rest of the year. My advice? Just enjoy it. It can be infectious if you let it."

"Like a virus," I murmured as she danced to the parade's music.

"What was that?" Gabe asked, leaning toward me.

"Nothing! Nothing."

* * *

Gabe urged me to take a leisurely bath, assuring me he and Pepper had the holiday preparations covered. I protested, offering to help, but they both nudged me upstairs.

"You've been working your butt off, Fortuna, taking care of everyone else. Let us handle this. We got it." She smiled at me warmly and tugged on my ratty bathrobe. "Promise. Go soak, get dressed in your party finery. We're good."

Party finery? I had a closet full of t-shirts and jeans. But I did as they directed, enjoying a long soak in my tub. I returned downstairs an hour and a half later in a clean t-shirt, new jeans, and makeup.

The makeup had to constitute party finery a little, right?

"You're just in time!" Pepper hollered. She grabbed my hand and yanked me over to the TV. "Here he comes! You almost missed it! I'm so glad you didn't miss it."

"Here who comes?" I asked, confused, as I stumbled across the room.

"Santa Claus!" she pointed excitedly as dozens of red and green sparkly dancers waved gigantic peppermint candies in a weird, diabetic-enthused dance. "It's Santa and Mrs. Claus! And the elves! And reindeer!" Pepper jumped up and down as a fat actor in a white beard waved to people lined up and down the street in front of Macy's in New York. "Are you excited? I'm so excited! It's Christmas! Officially! Right now, it's the Christmas season!" She jumped up and down and hugged me as if she'd just won the Pulitzer Prize.

The strange turn in the entire personality of my friend was leaving me breathless. I turned to find

Gabe looking at us, smiling. "Go with it," he mouthed silently and winked.

"Oh, I can't wait to decorate the tree," Pepper hugged me. She looked around. "Where is it?"

"Where's what?" I asked, smoothing down my shirt.

Her eyes narrowed. "The Christmas tree. Santa Claus just entered Herald Square. That act is the universally recognized starting shot for the Christmas season," she lectured me, her hands on her hips. "Now we have to put up the tree and decorate it. That's, like, the *whole* reason for Thanksgiving. So, where is it?"

"I don't have one. And that's not the whole reason for Thanksgiving," I told her, shaking my head. "It originated as a harvest festival. And now, you know, it's kind of controversial. Considering all of your views, I'm honestly surprised you even celebrate it."

Pepper crossed her arms. "Fortuna. Don't mess with my Thanksgiving."

"I'm just saying, Pepper, a lot of Native Americans see this as a day of mourning because—"

"Don't. Mess. With. My. Thanksgiving," Pepper warned me, her voice sharp. "This holiday is to gather with family, be thankful, eat food, and decorate the tree. The end. Where is the tree?"

"I'm just pointing out some people actually fast today, and there's a lot—"

"Gabe!" Pepper shouted at her ex-boyfriend. "Make her stop messing with my Thanksgiving!"

"If Fortuna feels differently about this, Pepper, I can't very well tell her not to," Gabe said, wiping his hands with a dishtowel. When he turned away from the range, I saw he was wearing an apron that said *Kiss The Cook*. "But she did invite us all over, so I think we're okay. She was just making a point. And for you, dear over-amped friend," Gabe leaned over and put his arm around Pepper, turning her. "Miss Bessie's entire Christmas stash, including the tree, is in those boxes over in that corner." Gabe pointed.

Pepper's face fell. "No *real* tree?"

"We're not killing a tree just to dress its dying corpse in drag for a month and then trash it," I told her. "I have to draw the line somewhere."

Pepper glared at me. "Witches," she said, tossing her head and diving into the boxes.

* * *

My house sparkled.

Blue and white tinsel draped from every possible place it could be draped without risking the whole house going up in flames. Glitter-covered snowflakes hung from the banister, walls, and exposed pipes, and turned my second floor into a winter wonderland. Pure white stockings hung by the chimney with our names written on them in silver. A six-foot green tree flocked with fake snow stood in the corner adorned with clear, silver, and blue balls interspersed with little glass icicles. White lights twinkled.

"This is awesome," Claire breathed as she came up the stairs. "Oh, Bella, isn't it beautiful?"

"I never thought I would have a holiday again. Yet here I am," the ghost answered quietly, her head swiveling. "Petey, say hello to your buddy, Gideon." Claire unclipped the greyhound's lead, and the two dogs ran into the kitchen and sniffed, looking for bacon.

"We're happy you could join us, Bella," Gabe said to the area next to Claire.

"Where's Spike?" Bella asked. Claire, after a few seconds, repeated the question.

"Liz had to do Evangeline Leroux's hair right before Thanksgiving dinner," Pepper made a sour face. "You know the great Clutterbuck princess. She has to outshine everyone everywhere she goes."

"It's all going to be smeared as soon as she gets near the booze, so I don't know what the point even is," I commented uncharitably about the former "movie star" (one gig as an extra) who seemed to

think she was the reincarnation of Marilyn Monroe
—from Monroe's *bad* years. Evangeline got away
with it because she was Chief Clutterbuck's
daughter. Still, even if he'd kept her shielded from
consequences so far, I suspected it wouldn't shield
her from the liver damage her copious booze habit
would cause.

"Have you ever seen what Liz does?" I shook
my head no at Pepper. "She sprays, like, a coat of
hair spray on her to keep things in place."

I raised an eyebrow. "What's weird about that?"

"On her face? Like, firehose-level hair spray. On
her *face*." Pepper turned to Gabe and raised an
eyebrow. "Hey, I just realized you're going to be the
only guy here."

"So?"

"Not true," I told Pepper. I grabbed a plate of
deviled eggs and set it out on the table. "Spike's
coming with Liz."

"Oh, I'm so glad," Claire smiled. "I definitely
want to tell him how thankful I am that he's been
hanging around with Bella and getting her
acclimated to...to, um..."

"Being dead?" Bella offered helpfully.

Claire's face fell as her own earbud carried her
ex-girlfriend's words.

"There will be none of that," Bella told her
sternly. After a few seconds, Claire nodded.

"Hey, let me help you hook up your phone to the speaker," I said, grabbing Claire's arm. "I got this so that the ghosts could participate a bit more in conversation. You just need to hook your phone up as a device, and your phone will broadcast what Bella's saying to everyone."

"Thanks."

Claire followed me over, and after a few stops and starts, her phone's sound came out of the speaker. "Won't this pick up all of them?" she asked.

"Maybe a stray word here and there," I shrugged. "But it seems like the app tunes itself the more you use it, so I think whoever people normally speak to will wind up coming through most clearly. Besides, you've all installed other voices, so everyone sounds slightly different, too."

Pepper ran over and handed us both a mug of Hot Buttered Apple Cider. When Pepper first explained the drink I wasn't particularly enthused to try it. But I have to hand it to Arkansans—adding butter and molasses to apple cider with a splash of bourbon and herbs was actually pretty darn tasty.

* * *

"First," Pepper said after we sat down to the immaculately set table. "I think we should all go around and say what we're thankful for." Gabe nodded and opened his mouth to speak, but Pepper cut him off. "I'll start," she glared, and his mouth closed.

"Petey, sit," Claire whispered to the greyhound next to her. Petey sat.

"This year has been a huge change for me," Pepper said, standing up. "I always knew there was something out there, something magical. Something more than what we see." She turned toward me and stared, her eyes shining. "But meeting Fortuna has shown me a glimpse of that other side. It's been the adventure of a lifetime."

A chorus of "Hear, hear" and "Absolutely" bubbled up from the table in agreement.

I blushed.

"But it's more than just meeting a real witch," she continued, glancing around the table and meeting everyone's eyes. "Every life and after-life around this table has been changed for the better because of Fortuna. Bella's murderer was brought to justice." Pepper waved toward Bella's ghost. "Petey was freed from the track and saved from who knows what. Gideon got his forever home. Gabe left the horrible police department and started his own detective agency. Spike's body was finally laid to rest, and Liz got her friend back. Miss Bessie finally found someone to pass her power down to, and because of Fortuna, Gabe didn't lose his grandmother when she moved on from this life. And I'm not even mentioning the things she—no, *we*—did for people not in this room. Together."

I could barely breathe as Pepper outlined all the things that had happened. I didn't know where to look, or what to do, or what to say. Out of the corner of my eye, I could see people—ghosts and humans —nodding.

"I got my first best friend back," Pepper said, staring at Gabe with love. "I never would have reconnected with Gabe if it wasn't for you, Fortuna. And he and I never would have realized that we were better as friends if we hadn't connected again through you."

"Oh, come on, guys," I whispered.

"No," Pepper said. "This group of people came together because of *you*. And this group is the group of friends I always wanted. Plus, Ollie," she smiled as she mentioned her absent boyfriend. "All of this —this dinner, this group, these relationships—it's all because of you. You're my best friend in the world. And I'm thankful for you."

Pepper hadn't tried to flatter me. Pepper never tried to flatter anyone. But her words had struck me to my core as I realized this group of people had become the family I never had. I tried to blink away tears, not sure how to accept the outpouring of love she had given me.

Just when I thought I couldn't take all the eyes on me, Pepper added snarkily, "The tree and decorations, though? That's *me.*" She jerked her thumb toward her chest. "And the dinner was Gabe. Because if we'd left this holiday dinner up to Fortuna, we *probably* would have all been eating bacon and cereal while sitting on the floor. She's good, but she's not *perfect.*"

Gideon and Petey jumped up and barked excitedly at the mention of bacon.

The group burst out laughing, and the spell of intensity was broken.

THREE

"Fortuna, you've got another reading here!" Claire shouted from the back of the shop as I made my way toward the front door hoping for a temporary escape. Turning, I craned my neck and spotted her jumping above the crowd, pointing. There were five people between the two of us, perusing the art hanging on the walls.

"I'm taking a break! I need some air!" I shouted, and turned away again to pick my way through a throng of people the likes of which I had never seen in my shop. There were so many looking for holiday gifts that Azalea and Gabe were tag-teaming behind the register as Claire tried to help people on the gallery floor. "I'll do some later this afternoon. Make an appointment for her!"

"Him!" she responded with a nod and turned back to speak to the customer.

"So much for long, leisurely days learning your magic." Miss Bessie floated through the tightly pressed assembly next to me. "I should have warned you about the holiday bazaar in the square. I know the Chamber of Commerce sent you a notice, but it didn't do the insanity justice. We're not going to get much done until after New Year's Day, I suspect." The old woman headed toward the front window and gazed out. "It *is* pretty, though. Don't you think?"

She was right, it was pretty.

A gigantic Christmas tree sparkled near the old courthouse on the lawn, and strings of lights covered the streets of the town square like a glittering gossamer net. A miniature train driven by an old man in an elf costume was circling excited children around the square. Hundreds of people milled around the streets on foot, looking at vendor stalls selling everything from jewelry to wreaths to apple cider.

"What an odd day to move in," Miss Bessie murmured.

I looked around. "What are you talking about?"

"Look, across the square," the ghost pointed. My gaze followed Miss Bessie's finger to find one of the closed storefronts on the other side lit up from within. A worker in blue overalls was applying letters to the front window in brown and gold while other uniformed, burly men drug stools and tables along the sidewalk. They carried them close, weaving between the throng of Christmas season celebrants as they headed toward the door. "Why bring those in the front?" she asked, frowning. "With the streets closed for the holidays, that makes no sense. That building must have a back entrance."

"You would think," I agreed.

We watched as a striking dark-haired woman walked out with Pepper following closely behind. The reporter held her notepad out and was diligently scribbling. After a few minutes, she closed the pad and shoved it in her satchel. The elegant woman stuck out her hand, and they shook.

With a skip, Pepper headed into the street and walked across the square toward my shop. I went outside to meet her.

"What's going on over there?" I asked her as she brushed fake snow from her hair.

"A new coffee shop. The woman's name is Dalida Dodd."

"Like the singer?"

"Um. Like the coffee shop owner," Pepper responded, pointing, without getting my reference to the famous French singer. "She says she's going to be open tomorrow, which is crazy. Yesterday that place was empty, with nothing in it. She's got an army of dudes in there cleaning, building, and setting up. Heck, you're a witch, and it took you two weeks to get your shop ready. It's impressive."

I glanced across the street, and within seconds the woman seemed to sense I was watching her. She turned toward us and tilted her head, then raised her hand and waved elegantly. I waved back in my mother's distant style—a simple open and close of my hand. "Where's she from?"

Pepper handed me a brown coffee cup and pulled out her pad. She flipped through her notes. "Huh. How about that," she murmured after scanning three pages. "I didn't even ask her. I must be all discombobulated from the holidays. There's a reason I don't do any investigative reporting this time of year."

Miss Bessie and I glanced at one another. "You didn't ask her where she was from?"

"I guess not. Oh, well," Pepper said, smiling. "It's not really important. She's here now." That she didn't remember to ask such a fundamental question necessary for a new business profile didn't seem to bother her.

"I think I ought to go on over there and check this newcomer out," Miss Bessie said with a deeper frown. "The day Pepper Stanford forgets to ask someone a Journalism 101 question on a puff piece is a day all of us should be concerned. Be right back."

I nodded to Miss Bessie and watched her float through the holiday crowd. Lifting the coffee cup, I looked at the logo—*The Golden Cup Coffee House*. The golden yellow cup on the logo reminded me— vaguely—of cups on a tarot card. As I examined it, Pepper snatched it back out of my hand and gulped it.

"You should go try her coffee," Pepper told me after swallowing. "I don't know what kind of caffeine is in it, but it's fantastic. I feel almost lighter." She giggled and took another sip.

"Is she open? They're still lugging in furniture," I pointed out.

"She has coffee already. Well, not to sell, but you're neighbors! You should go say hi!"

"Maybe later," I told her, nodding.

Now it was my turn to sense someone watching me. I turned back and looked across the square to find that Dalida Dodd hadn't moved from her doorway.

Not one inch.

* * *

"Fortuna?"

I looked up to find Jeeves standing in the

hallway outside my new private office/parlor. "Afternoon," I told him cautiously as I set down shipping labels I had been preparing. "What brings you to Christmas Central?"

"You think this is bad? You haven't been up to the complex yet." Jeeves slipped in and closed the door behind him. "Ask Pepper, I saw her at the casino earlier. The square is definitely festive, but I venture a guess that Martin's decorations could give the square a run for the town's money."

"That's a funny phrase to use," I said, sitting down. "Considering how you all make all your money."

"Not all."

"Too much. It shouldn't be any," I deadpanned.

"This is off to a good start, I see." The vampire sat down across from me and stared.

Martin and Jeeves were determined to manipulate me into finding the witch bottles hidden around Mystic's End (bottles that contained the spirits of the town's founding coven members and/or their descendants). I was just as determined to use their need of me to get them to end greyhound racing at their entertainment complex on the edge of town.

It could make conversations between us a little tedious and snippy.

"I just don't think you two have made enough

progress on the plan to end greyhound racing, Jeeves."

"I'm not here to talk about that," Jeeves began again after a pause.

I raised an eyebrow. "Then what are you here to talk about?"

"Martin Salvatore," Jeeves said, referencing Martin's mafia don father.

I rolled my eyes. "And what do I need to know about the Dreamboat Don this Thanksgiving weekend?" I wasn't in the mood to be tied to Martin as much as I was, I didn't want to add Marty Salvatore to the list. In fact, I had hoped to avoid Martin *and* Jeeves the entire holiday month thanks to the unexpected visit from the magical mob.

"I think he's here because of you."

I sat up and blinked. That got my attention. "What do you mean?"

"Martin and his father are not particularly close, but they do—obviously—have business ties. For the most part, Mr. Salvatore is quite content to simply look at spreadsheets and bank statements. He rarely visits Martin, and Martin barely visits him. One of the benefits, I suppose, of having magical creatures on staff."

"I still don't see what this has to do with me. Besides, Jeeves, maybe he's just getting older, and he wanted to visit his son? Sure, he's a mob boss, but he's also a father."

"And maybe the people he's planted here have caught wind of the fact that Martin is looking for the spirit of his mother," Jeeves countered.

"What about Uncle Vito?" I asked him, referencing Martin's great-uncle, Vito Salvatore. "Maybe he just talked to his nephew, and they wanted to get together for the holidays. It's not like Uncle Vito is young. It could be a simple thing. Like Vito was too old or ill to travel," I told him, reaching for a perfectly innocent explanation. "It's the holiday season, Jeeves. Don't be so paranoid."

The vampire stared at me, his eyes narrowing. "I get paid to be paranoid."

"Wait, you get *paid*?" I exclaimed in mock shock. "In something other than blood? Really? Is that a new thing?" I pushed back on my chair as we stared at one another, and dove into yet another long, uncomfortable silence.

He was the one to break it. "You hold on to things for an amazing amount of time, Miss Delphi."

"I remember what I need to remember, so I don't get manipulated," I shot back, leaning forward. My tone was more annoyed than I intended it to be, but the fact that Gabe and Pepper had called Jeeves to help with the range had irked me. We were not friends, me and the vampire—and I wanted Jeeves to be *perfectly clear* that we were not friends. "You two played me once already. Heck, you, yourself, played me all on your own. I make mistakes once, vampire. Only once. You don't get to mess with my head twice."

"Is that why you moved the private detective into your shop?" His eyebrow rose as he shifted on the hard chair, and he gestured toward the door dismissively. "To ensure that Martin won't feel comfortable coming here?"

"Hey, bub, I don't need anyone to protect me from Martin," I told him fiercely. "I can do that all on my own, unlike him—since he needs you and a stable of Daddy's witches to wrap him in cotton like a china doll. And who *I* move into *my* shop is none of your damn business. It's none of his, either."

Jeeves and I stared at one another, his face insufferably calm, and mine flushed with indignation. Finally, he sighed. "Look, I didn't come here to upset you. The fact is this all may be my fault," he said, his voice wavering. "My idea for you to fake the vision that helped catch Bella's murder could have galvanized Don Salvatore's concern. I did not expect it would wind up on the front page of the newspaper."

"Why was that a big deal?" I asked him.

"It was a big deal because I was standing over

you," Jeeves explained. "And Martin was at the table. And that photo—with the two of us in it—was on the front page of the paper." He could not keep the edge out of his voice despite how naturally adept he was at hiding all emotions (assuming he had any). "A paper that Don Salvatore saw eventually. I told you once that we did not want him to know about you."

"But now he does," I said.

"Now he does," Jeeves nodded, relief on his face that I seemed to understand the predicament he and Martin were in. "And he now knows Martin is acquainted with a psychic medium, one he never mentioned to his father."

I examined him for a moment, trying to process what he was telling me. "He doesn't know I'm a witch, though?"

"No, he does not. But I suspect that is why he is here. To find out if you are and to find out why Martin seems to be acquainted with you."

"Why would he care?" Jeeves frowned and didn't answer. "Look, dude, if you want to make this my problem, you have to trust me with what's going on. I don't even get, at this point, why you're telling me all this."

"I'm telling you this because if Marty Salvatore thinks his son is trying to oust him as Don with your help, you are in danger." He tilted his head. "We all are."

"Why would he think that?" I asked. Jeeves stared back. My eyes widened. "Oh, you *have* to be kidding me." Martin was secretly trying to overthrow his own father?

"Nothing's...certain," Jeeves said quietly. "No action has been taken, nothing has been done. But we are dealing with a man that can pull thoughts out of the heads of men. Some of what Martin has done and is doing could be seen as a betrayal."

"Then why did you just come here and tell me all this!" I shouted, throwing a squeeze stress ball at the vampire. Dear Lord, did these two just enjoy roping people into their cloak-and-dagger games for funsies? None of this was my problem, and suddenly, because of a photograph in a newspaper, the whole thing was.

Jeez, these two annoyed me.

"Your gemstone protects you against more than just me," Jeeves said, nodding toward my hidden magic-blocking stone stuffed uncomfortably into my bra.

"What stone?" I asked innocently.

Jeeves straightened the wrinkles on his jacket, then stood up. His voice rode the edge of calmly controlled and frustrated as he looked down at me.

"Normally, I find the games I play with you quite amusing, Fortuna, but at the moment, I don't have time." The corner of his left eye twitched, something I'd never seen before. "Marty Salvatore is clever, too clever by far. Be careful. Be wary of any new people that come into your life. Your telepathy cannot be sensed, but your magic will be. Don't use it."

"Okay, I've got it," I told him, standing up. "You told me on the phone last night, and I said I'd keep it under wraps. Besides, this town's been invaded by tourists, and now they're everywhere. I'm not going to be using magic for a bit—though I gotta tell you, I'm now wasting an awful lot of paint with these readings."

"This is serious," he said, his mouth tightening.

"I *said* I got it!"

Jeeves stared at me intently, his eyes holding mine. "I know you don't care about us, and I understand you're angry with us. But if Martin's plans are discovered, Fortuna, the track will go into someone else's hands. I guarantee you those hands will not be as gentle. Nor will you be able to convince whoever is put in charge to end greyhound racing. So," he pointed out blandly. "If you hold any hope of freeing all those dogs at the track, it would behoove you to help us keep these secrets from Don Salvatore."

"I said I would," I responded slowly. "How

many more times do you need me to say it? Any other guilt trip or manipulation or veiled threat you feel like tossing my way? You know, just to *really* twist the screws?"

The vampire's mouth turned up in a half-smile. "Happy holidays, Fortuna," Jeeves said dryly, making his way to the door.

"You're such a jerk sometimes," I called after him.

I felt caught in a vise.

Again.

* * *

B e wary of any new people that come into your life.

I stood on the sidewalk and stared across the square at *The Golden Cup Coffee House.*

Dalida Dodd, shadowed by Miss Bessie's ghost, glanced over and waved again.

FOUR

Saturday morning was twice as bad as Friday. "Okay, guys, line up orderly, so I can fill out the paperwork for your paintings!" I shouted at the students milling around the back studio. We had sold so much art on Friday that Pepper and I spent Friday night calling every student I had to ask them if they had any pieces to sell. It was, admittedly, a good problem to have, but the walls of the *Mystic Moon Gallery* were nearly bare. "We need to get them stickered, numbered, and priced out!"

"Do you need help?" Pepper asked as she walked in from the front.

"I need a drink," I mumbled.

"You don't really drink, though," she pointed out with an eyebrow raised.

"I might start." I handed her a pack of pre-numbered stickers and a pen. "Can you just go down the line and sticker each piece? That way, when they get up here, it will take me less time to record the artist and..." I swiveled around, looking for a pen. "Where's my pen? Where the heck did my pen go?"

Pepper held up the pen I just handed her, her face suffused with concern. "Has she been like this all morning, Gideon?" my friend asked my dog, who was sleeping on a pile of scraps just behind me. He raised his long head wearily and looked up at Pepper with one eye half-open. Then he yawned with a small whine. Then he lowered his head, sighed loudly, and went back to sleep. "Well, fine, don't talk to me, then."

"He's annoyed because I didn't have time to take him to the dog park this morning. Just ignore him."

Gideon's head shot up, his eyes narrowed, and my head filled with images of bacon.

"Oh, right," I remembered. "And I ran out of bacon. So, he's in a bit of a huff today."

"No one's allowed to have a bad day during the happy season," Pepper told both of us. She handed me back the pen, then pulled a handful from her satchel. "Here. Now you can't run out of pens. One problem solved." Next, she pulled out her phone, and her thumbs flew over the screen. "And the second problem solved. Ollie will swing by with a package of bacon."

Gideon shot up and barked at her frantically.

"Two?" she asked him.

The barking did not let up.

"How about a deep freeze and a case of bacon? Would *that* quiet you down, greedy?"

Gideon raced over and pressed his muscular body against Pepper's leg, his head happily bobbing up and down on her thigh.

"Go lay down. You'll get your bacon," Pepper told him, snapping her fingers and pointing to his makeshift bed. "And be nicer to Fortuna. Her business pays for your bacon, bub. Even Gabe is working the register to help out. So chill with the attitude, huh?"

Gideon barked once, shot me a glare that would have terrified a rabbit, and then settled back down for his leisurely morning nap once again. Despite Aunt Pepper's dog lecture, Gideon was not thrilled with me.

"Thanks for trying," I told her as I stacked up the consignment paperwork. "Okay, let's get to stickering and processing. I can't sell them if they're not on the wall."

* * *

The back studio was quiet once again after I processed almost thirty artists and four times the number of art pieces. Because it was so quiet, it was suddenly easy to observe that Uncle Vito arrived with three men dressed in identical suits, and one taller man.

Uncle Vito, Martin's great-uncle (and the uncle of his mafia father, Don Salvatore), was the last artist in line. And to my chagrin, the taller man standing just slightly behind him was impeccably dressed—and bore a striking resemblance to Martin Salvi.

I had not called Uncle Vito.

On purpose.

Apparently, Pepper did.

Great.

"Fortuna, honey, how ya doin'? You look like you been gummed up by the hammer and saws!" The old man strolled up and placed several canvases down.

"I've been...I'm sorry, what?" Uncle Vito spoke like a villain from a Dick Tracy comic strip. It was endearing in a way. The problem is a good portion of the time I had no idea what he was talking about.

"The coppers, the coppers, you look like they put you through somethin', that's all." Uncle Vito reached out and gave me a quick hug. "The news-hawk over there called me and told me you needed more stuff, so I brought you five of my best." He held up five canvases, all in vibrant, happy colors. "I could use some scratch to bet on the big game, anyway, so it's good. It's good." He nodded and held them out.

"Uncle Vito, aren't you going to introduce me?" asked the handsome older man behind him. He was dressed in a crisp white shirt and a dark suit, clearly expensive. His black cap-toe oxfords were shined to a near mirror finish. His outfit was finished with a long coat and a hat that covered his salt-and-pepper hair, pulled just slightly to the side. "You've told me so much about your art instructor. I would love to make her formal acquaintance."

Martin's father spoke about me as if I wasn't even there, but his eyes bore into mine. Clearly, stares of unusual intensity are inheritable traits.

I pushed myself off the stool to shake hands, and the two silent men stepped forward swiftly, their hands reaching toward their waistbands. I halted. So did they. Glancing at them both, I wondered if they were vampires like Jeeves. Would vampire bodyguards even need to carry guns?

"Marty, this is Fortuna Delphi. Fortuna, my brother's kid, Marty Salvatore," Uncle Vito announced cheerfully. I kept my face impassive despite my surprise. Vito knew quite well that "Marty's" son and I were acquainted with one another. I marked that he did not mention Martin at all when making the introduction.

"Mr. Salvatore, it's a pleasure to meet you," I nodded as I extended my hand. He clasped it firmly as we shook. "Your uncle is a wonderful student. Truly, one of my most talented."

"You are a true saint, Miss Delphi, volunteering to teach people at the old folks home." Don Salvatore did not release my hand when we finished shaking. Instead, he pulled his other hand forward and covered mine, clutching my hand just tight enough I couldn't pull away without yanking my hand. "Not many people take time to give the elderly the attention and care they have earned throughout a lifetime." The two men behind him relaxed their stance and stepped back, though both still eyed me warily.

"Not at all, sir."

"Is that a racing greyhound I see behind you?" The elder Salvatore leaned around me and eyed Gideon—who was clearly a terrible watchdog. The dog snored as I entertained the Dreamboat Don in my studio. "What a stunning animal." He smiled knowingly at me. "Have you ever raced him?"

"No," I answered more harshly than I intended. "Gideon's retired."

I glanced over at Pepper and was shocked to find she was paying absolutely no attention to the mafia boss, the exchange we were having, or the two men that almost pulled weapons in my art studio because I got up too fast. If her quiet laughs and the sound coming from her speakers were any indications, she was watching cat videos. Did my conspiracy-theorist friend just become brain dead for the Christmas season?

"That's a shame." Don Salvatore turned from the still sleeping Gideon. His eyes swept the room casually, but he seemed to be looking for something. "With thighs like that, I bet he's incredibly fast."

"This is as fast as he goes most of the time," I answered. "He seems to be happier in retirement."

"Oh?" The older man perked up, his eyes alight as he turned around. "Did he tell you that?" The two men to either side of him tensed and concentrated on me.

If they were trying to read me, I couldn't feel it. If they were scanning me, it didn't make enough of a blip to register. And they, like Martin, were telepathically unreadable. It felt like the room grew several degrees warmer as their focus on me blazed.

But Uncle Vito was not telepathically unreadable—at least not with the iron-clad strength they were—and I heard the faint whisper of,

"Careful, girlie." A clouded, foggy feeling of concern emanated from the old man.

"Any dog would be happier to lay around all day, play in a dog park, and sun themselves if the alternative is living in a cage with periodic sprints in a circle chasing a lure," I told the man.

"Not a fan of the track, are you?" he asked with a smirk of malicious amusement.

"No, sir."

He stared at me with an almost hypnotic intensity, and I again wondered *what the heck* was wrong with Pepper that she happily grinned at her screen—while I stared down an uncoiling cobra five feet from her. Don Salvatore's gaze was one of the coldest I'd ever had the misfortune to be on the receiving end of.

And then, suddenly, he was warm and exuding a faux affection, his face brightened by a devilish grin. I heard Uncle Vito exhale as Marty Salvatore nodded. "Well, if you've finished with my uncle, we have family business to attend to. Miss Delphi, it was wonderful to meet you." I was grateful he did not reach out to shake my hand.

I swallowed and nodded. "I'll get these up in the front within the next few days, Uncle Vito." I placed the canvases gently with the others.

"You check out that fourth one," he said. The

four men headed toward the back. "There's a depth to it I really like."

"Will do!" I called as he walked out the door.

As the metal back door slammed, Pepper looked up. "Oh, are we finished?"

"Are you drunk?" I gaped at her in disbelief.

"Of course not, it's not even lunchtime yet," she said, slamming her laptop closed. Looking around the studio, she frowned. "There's no decorations in here. You should decorate the art studio for the holidays, Fortuna. It's not festive in here at all."

"Did you notice *anything* that just happened?" I asked her.

"A bunch of people brought art. You're going to sell it. What's to notice?"

Sheer amazement probably wasn't even close to what I felt as I stared at her.

* * *

"Look, she does get a little loopy during the holidays," Gabe said after I told him what occurred in the back with Uncle Vito, Don Salvatore, and Pepper, the oblivious cat-video watcher. "But the guy is a mafia kingpin or something. I imagine he practices intensity in the mirror before bed. If you were in any danger at all,

I'm sure Gideon would have alerted to it. Isn't he your familiar or something?"

"He's mad at me," I told him with a defiant pout.

"Run out of bacon?"

I glared.

Gabe smiled. "Well, while you were in the back starring in your own Mystic's End version of *The Godfather*, Azalea and I sold almost every piece of art not nailed down. We actually had to close the shop to clear people out so we could restock." Gabe glanced at the newly delivered pieces. "Yeah, that might last a few days tops. Can't you magic up a few more?"

"Shhhhhhhhh!" I leaned into the hallway and made sure Azalea was out of earshot. "I don't want that kid to know anything more than she does. It's enough that she works for the crazy psychic hippie lady. Let's not let her know it's more than that."

Gabe and I both jumped as loud banging echoed down the corridor. He turned frowning. "What the—" he muttered, hurrying toward the front. I followed "Weird. Is Joe Bellinger a customer of yours?"

"Who?" I asked, confused.

"Joe Bellinger. He works in Little Rock, but he lives in town." Gabe hurried to the door where a heavyset, angry man was beating on the glass door with a balled fist. "Joe, what on earth—"

"You gotta investigate the wife," Mr. Bellinger said, storming into the shop. Gabe slammed the front door shut and locked it before the tourists could follow. "There's something wrong with her. Something serious. You gotta do something about it!"

Azalea stared at the man, stiffening.

"Joe, I'm a private investigator. I find out about things, but I don't do anything about what I find," Gabe explained as the man paced. "I can't, I'm not with the police anymore. Why don't you calm down and tell me what the problem is?"

"It's Harriet!" he shouted with a damning scowl. "She's happy. So happy! That woman is flitting through life on a pocket of cotton-candy air that's blowing between her ears!"

"You want to hire Gabe because your wife is... happy?" I asked in disbelief.

"Have you *met* Harriet?" he asked me, his scowl deepening.

"No, sir."

"That woman is the most critical, unhappy, unsatisfiable woman that God ever placed upon his blessed green earth, ma'am," Joe Bellinger told me. He pulled a bandanna from his back pocket and wiped the sweat from his brow. "She hates this town. She hates our house. She hates our kids. She hates the other ladies at church. Hell, most of the time, that woman hates *me*," he insisted.

I smiled sympathetically. "Mr. Bellinger, I'm *sure* hate is a strong word," I told him, but he cut me off.

"Have you *met my wife?*" he bellowed at me. I shook my head no. "Nothing makes her happy. In forty years, miss, *nothing* has cracked that woman's judgmental statue of a face. No one in this town has ever seen her damn teeth besides the dentist!"

Gabe nodded and placed a hand on Joe's shoulder, trying to calm the man down. "And now she's...?"

"Not her! She's just not!" Bellinger cried, throwing his calloused hands in the air. "She loves everybody. And everything! Our kid came home and told us he was quitting college to start a rock band—nothin'! She just smiled! Our other kid wrecked my pickup truck yesterday—she didn't care! It's like she's one of them pod people!" he exclaimed animatedly. Turning to Gabe, he begged, "You gotta help me, son. It ain't normal. It ain't normal! I can't live like this!"

I turned back and looked at Pepper, who was happily finger painting a smiley face and giggling.

"Okay, Joe, why don't we sit down," Gabe said to the man.

Joe blinked and nodded. "There's something wrong, I tell ya. My whole life done turned upside down!" he finished, panting. "Can you help me, Gabe? I got a Christmas bonus. I can pay ya." He sat down with a thump on the couch, and his face fell. "I loved my wife just the way she was, Wilcox," Joe said quietly, his eyes filling with tears. "I know everyone thinks she's a hard woman, but she's my woman. And I love her. You gotta help me get my wife back, Wilcox."

Gabe and I looked at one another, and then he turned to Joe Bellinger. "No problem, Joe. Let's start at the beginning. When did you first notice your wife was happy?"

FIVE

Pepper was even worse on Sunday than she was on Saturday.

"What is she *doing*?" Azalea whispered before the gallery's opening, her eyes wide as she watched an ebullient Pepper toss tinsel up in the air. My studio was covered with the stuff. "She knows that we can't leave that all over the place, right? Gideon might eat it and get sick." Glancing at the clock, Azalea announced she was getting the wet/dry vacuum out.

Turning back to Pepper, I heard keys jingle from the front. Gabe called out a hearty good morning.

"Gabe!" Pepper screeched. She ran from the studio into the corridor at breakneck speed, still clutching her fistfuls of silver tinsel. "Gabe, my buddy, my pal, my old friend! Have some tinsel!" Instead of handing it to him, she threw one fistful up in the air and rained it down upon his head. "Ooh, you look so good with the tinsel. *So* good with the tinsel! Look at how handsome you are," she cooed happily.

"Well, she's one bubble off plumb, ain't she?" Miss Bessie remarked as she floated in.

"Where have *you* been? You went off to check out the new coffee shop woman on Friday. It's now Sunday. I don't think you know what *right back* means anymore."

"What's two days within an eternity? I got nothing but time now, and you're not doing anything but working, anyway," Miss Bessie shrugged. Pointing at the giggling, dancing Pepper, she asked, "What in tarnation is wrong with that girl?"

Azalea walked by the four of us, rolling the shop vac and cast a questioning look at me. Out of everyone regularly in the shop, only poor Azalea was unaware of the constant arrival, and exit of the town's dearly departed residents from my gallery. I avoided Miss Bessie's question and turned to Gabe.

"Gabe, is this like Pepper's other...um, holiday episodes?"

He glanced at Pepper and turned, shaking his

head no. "This is something different. And what's more? It's not only Pepper." He took a swig from a water bottle. "It's happening to other people in the town."

"Mrs. Bellinger?" I guessed.

"Mrs. Bellinger, Dexter Kane, a few people at the old folks home."

"Who?" Miss Bessie asked curiously.

After a pause, Gabe answered. "Harold Whatnow is one. Someone else named Judy?"

"Harold Whatnow is *happy*? You must be mistaken, boy. Harold is never happy," the ghost scoffed. "Harold was born sorry, and just evolved his mad over time until it was honed. He's as friendly as a bramble bush. That man is never happy," she insisted, and then she paused. "Well, *I've* seen him happy. But only for about five minutes at a time every Wednesday," Miss Bessie said. Then she sighed dreamily. "Was a great five minutes, though."

Gabe's cheeks crimsoned brightly as the words made their way from the ghost to his phone and, finally, to his earbud. "Anyway," he said quickly. "It all started in the past couple of days."

"Right when that new coffee shop opened up," I blurted out.

"What new coffee shop?" Gabe asked.

"Come on, I'll show you," I waved at him and

walked toward the front gallery. "It was a little weird. On Thursday, nothing. On Friday, they moved in. By Saturday morning, they were open. I doubt a lot of small businesses could have done what she did in the time she did it." I pointed across the square to show Gabe—and gasped in disbelief.

The line for Dalida Dodd's shop was out the door and stretched halfway down the block.

"That place opened just *yesterday*?" Gabe asked, staring in amazement. "That's one heck of a crowd for a one-day-old coffee shop."

"I know, right? Your grandmother went over there to check it out."

"Did she find out anything?"

"It's a coffee shop." Miss Bessie floated over. "Fancy machines, beans in bags, paper cups. Nothing looked out of the ordinary at all. I eavesdropped all day. Still don't know where she came from since brain dead over there"—Miss Bessie waved toward Pepper, who was now sitting on the floor trying to convince Gideon he should dress up like Rudolf for the holidays—"decided not to bother asking the question. But nothing struck me as out of sorts."

"It's *got* to be her," I told Gabe.

He frowned. "How do you figure? I don't have any indication Miss Belligerent...um, Mrs. Bellinger went to the coffee shop at all. She doesn't drink caffeine."

I raised an eyebrow. "Miss Belligerent?"

Gabe shifted uneasily. "That's her nickname at the church. Mr. Bellinger wasn't kidding about her being abrasive. She's notorious for it. Anyway, while I agree with you that it's a little suspicious some folks are suddenly happy-go-lucky when it's not their nature, I don't think we can automatically assume that Dalida Dodd is, like, putting something in their coffee. What would even *do* that, anyway?"

"It seems to me that Pepper started acting a bit bonkers when she came back from the interview. And though it's not like she's drunk or woozy," I said, staring at my friend who lay on the floor. "It's not like she's normal, either. Something's clearly going on."

"I'm going to call Ollie," Gabe said, pulling out his phone. "One, he might have an idea of what this could be, and that will give me a better idea of what I'm looking for. Two, that's his girlfriend," Gabe said as his fingers swiped through his contacts. "Ollie should know what's going on."

* * *

"Sorry, folks! We're sold out!" I shouted after climbing on top of the counter. The storefront was packed with smiling, happy customers shoulder to shoulder waving money. "If you need art supplies, please move carefully up to the front toward the counter. If you're looking for local art to buy, we're out today. We might have some more pieces tomorrow."

A groan went up from the crowd as hands came down and bodies turned to head toward the door.

"This is insane," I mumbled as I climbed down and jumped onto the floor. Azalea raised an eyebrow at me. "I feel like I'm making up for all those months I had trouble getting this business going. I couldn't even do any readings today."

As the last customer headed out the door, my assistant raced to place a canvas in the window. She had quickly prepared one informing people we were selling supplies only. Another canvas quickly followed, telling people they should check back tomorrow for local art.

It wasn't in the window for three seconds before a boorish woman pushed in the door on a mission. "Is that for sale?" she pointed to the sign Azalea had just placed. "I'll give you a hundred dollars for it. I love the colors!"

"Ma'am, that's just a store sign," I told her politely. "It's just letting you know that there's no more art for sale today. We'll try and have more tomorrow."

"But you've only been open three hours!" she huffed, pointing at the hours sign.

"I understand," I nodded and smiled. "We sold out early. There was a higher demand than we anticipated. If you check back tomorrow, I'm sure we'll have—"

"Sell that to me! That's art!" she demanded again and pulled wads of cash from her purse. Gabe's eyes narrowed as he watched. The woman was almost breathless with excitement, her eyes shining.

"No, ma'am, that's a *sign*," I disagreed, speaking slowly. "I assure you, we will work on getting our inventory topped up and should have more pieces—"

"Okay, two hundred dollars!" she shouted with a bubbly exuberance.

Gabe and I looked at one another.

I engaged with the woman back and forth, all the way up to an offer of five hundred dollars for Azalea's hastily painted sign before she gave up and left. She didn't seem disappointed at all and walked swiftly toward another store, cash still in hand.

"I'm going to go paint," Azalea announced. "If that woman was going to pay that much for a sign, I need to *Morris Katz* this stuff. I could pay for a year of college off this holiday season, easy." She frowned and grabbed five canvases. Then ten. "I'll be back for more," she murmured as she raced down the corridor toward the studio hugging the blank cloth squares. Pepper jumped up and ran after her.

"Who's Morris Katz?" Gabe asked, confused.

"The world's fastest painter. Set a world record, too—complete painting in just thirty seconds. He did a benefit once and painted one hundred and three paintings in twelve hours," I told him. "He called his works *Instant Art*. Obviously, he was pretty prolific."

"Huh. Are they worth anything?"

"You can get some of his stuff at auction for a few hundred dollars. Some are worth a few thousand. Some sell for less than a hundred on eBay. He has a lot of stuff."

"One down!" Azalea called from the back.

"Back to the subject at hand." Gabe leaned against the counter and folded his muscular forearms across his chest. "Hopefully, Ollie can give us a clue what to look for when he gets here. What just happened here? That's not normal. I'm sure Azalea's art is nice and all, but no one bids up a store sign. It's not an Andy Warhol."

I smiled. "You just named the only famous artist you knew, didn't you?"

"It's not the *only* one I know." He raised his chin defiantly. "I know about Picasso. Chagall. The...the guy with the melting clocks."

I snickered. "You mean Salvador Dali?"

"Yeah, him."

The store was quiet, almost peaceful, after the insanity of the morning.

"Do you like Dali's work?" I asked as I grabbed a rag and wiped all the fingerprints off my counter. "Or Warhol's?"

"The melting clocks are cool. Hey, what do they mean? Do you know?"

"People have hypothesized different things. That time isn't relative or fixed. That they represent the time, we lose while asleep. Someone even guessed it might have to do with Einstein's Theory of Relativity, which was groundbreaking in the thirties—Dali might have been making a statement about the relationship between space and time," I explained. Gabe watched me quietly, listening. "If you want to know what Dali *himself* said about his inspiration? It was a melted wheel of cheese."

"I'm sorry, did you say a melted wheel of *cheese?*"

I nodded. "Profound art can be inspired by pretty mundane things. Or Dali could have been pulling everyone's leg." I smiled. "You can see in a work whatever it is that you want to see. No one can tell you what it means to you."

"Done!" Azalea shouted again.

"Hey, Azalea, is Pepper okay back there?" I called.

"She's not here! Maybe she went upstairs!"

Gabe and I looked at each other with matching frowns.

Then we locked the store door and raced upstairs.

But she was gone.

* * *

"So, y'all lost my definitely crazy-acting, possibly drugged girlfriend, is what you're saying," Ollie said after hearing our story. His demeanor was quintessential Ollie. He leaned back and looked us both up and down, his long hair in a ponytail that trailed down his shoulder. "Just *ignored* her to sell paintings and chat about art. Okay, you own the shop"—Ollie pointed at me—"but *you*, brother, are a detective. Maybe there was a little more to the chief firing you than you just disobeying orders on a bad day? Maybe?"

"Ollie, I—"

"I'm just saying, Gabe, that if it was your girlfriend acting all drugged and crazy-like, I would have kept track of her—know what I mean?" Ollie leaned forward and leveled a flat gaze at Gabe.

"I don't have a girlfriend," Gabe told Ollie,

cutting a quick side glance at me—even though his comment did not pertain to any discussion we were having at the moment.

"Now, see, *I'm* thinking you may want to explore why that is." Ollie's angular face clouded with concern as he looked up at Gabe from the couch. "When you do, you give me a call, brother. I'll be happy to help get across to you why that might be."

"I think we're getting off the subject here," I broke in.

Ollie stood up swiftly, his hard shoulder driving into Gabe's ribcage. The detective, who had been standing over his best friend, doubled over with an *oomph*. I couldn't tell whether it was an accident or on purpose, but Ollie seemed satisfied with himself.

"Okay, folks, how're we going to find her?" Ollie looked at me. "How did you find her in the woods that time when Bill took her?"

"Six done!" Azalea shouted from the back.

I blinked. "I don't know. Spike just told me I should try things, and I...I think I left my body and looked around, and there was a light shining from the direction of the forest." I shrugged. "I followed it, and there she was."

"So try again," Ollie told me.

Spike floated through the wall I shared with

Liz's salon and greeted everyone. "I heard my name. What's up?"

"Pepper is missing. Ollie just wanted me to try what I did when Bill had her to see if we can locate her."

Spike blinked. "Pepper's not missing," he said, confused. "She's next door getting her hair done."

"On a Sunday? Liz isn't even open, is she?"

"Well, no, but it's Pepper, right?" Spike smiled. "Liz and I were just watching a movie, and Pepper was real insistent about wanting her hair done for the holidays. Miss Bessie's over there, too."

"She's next door," I told the guys. Turning, I shouted toward the studio. "Azalea, we're going to run next door for a minute! I'm going to leave the front door locked, but you might want to listen for a knock!"

"Eight! And okay!" she shouted back.

The four of us—three humans and a ghost—made our way to Liz's hair salon, *Magic Cuts*. We took longer than usual to walk one store down because of the incredible crush of humanity that celebrated with jolly merriment in every direction. It seemed as if the number of people in the square had doubled in a day.

Without thinking, I reached out and wiggled my index finger to unlock Liz's front door, ushering Ollie and Gabe in behind me. It was only after I closed the door I remembered my promise to Jeeves not to use magic—and the cold stare of Marty Salvatore as he visited.

Shoot.

"Are you okay? You suddenly look a little pale," Gabe asked.

I looked up into his eyes and forced a smile. "I'm good."

"Hello?" Liz called from behind the wall that separated the waiting area from the stations. Ollie ran toward the back with Gabe and me following.

"What the—" Ollie burst out. He stopped his advance toward his girlfriend cold and stared at her in horror. "Oh, baby, what on earth did you do?"

"It's Christmas!" she shouted and smiled at Ollie in the mirror. Liz turned the chair, tense, and presented our friend, Pepper Stanford. Serious reporter. Occult investigator. Brilliant researcher.

And an honorary member of the Lollipop Guild.

"She was insistent," Liz said, stepping back. "I tried to talk her out of it, but it is *her* hair. I don't tell women what they should or shouldn't do with their hair. Well, I mean,"—Liz tilted her head—"once they listen to me tell them what to do, and they decide to ignore it, I don't."

"I've had worse," Spike said with a shrug.

I couldn't imagine how.

Pepper's long, beautiful blond locks were cut short, and the hair chunked into dyed red stripes. The bright, fire engine red was interspersed with hair bleached so light it looked white. She looked like a walking peppermint candy.

"Please tell me that's a wig," I begged Liz.

"Please tell me that's not permanent," Gabe breathed.

"Don't you love it, Ollie? Isn't it beautiful?" Pepper asked happily, her face glowing. She appeared oblivious to our horrified reactions, and clearly over the moon about her festive new do.

Ollie took a deep breath and walked over to gather her in his arms. "You look beautiful, sweetie," he said, and he kissed her gently. "Absolutely beautiful."

She squealed happily and buried her smiling face in his chest.

While Pepper hugged him and giggled, Ollie looked back at us and dropped the supportive mask he'd forced himself to wear. His face was lined with concern.

And fear.

SIX

"And in our top story this evening, a homeowner in Grigio Hills is in hot water today after a holiday pool party brought complaints from neighbors and caused thousands of dollars in property damage," the television Gabe brought announced. "That, and more, when we return."

"A pool party!" Pepper shrieked, rocking back and forth excitedly. "Oh, how did I miss a Christmas pool party!"

"Mystic's End has its own local news show? Why did I not know this?" I asked Gabe as Ollie tried to calm Pepper down. "Aren't we part of the Little Rock area?"

"You didn't know this because you didn't have a television," Gabe said as he cooked dinner.

"Hey, I had a television," I pointed to the small, square box sitting under Gabe's gigantic big screen. "I even rigged it so Gideon could stream movies for Spike by pressing buttons. See?" I walked over and stepped on a plastic button. The button clicked, and the tiny TV turned on.

"Okay, you didn't have a *real* television. That's not really a television. That's an antique," Gabe disagreed. "And you didn't have cable. This is a cable station."

"But I *don't* have cable."

"You do now." Gabe smiled and pointed to the cable box attached to his television. "I ordered it for my office so I could keep up with the news, and I ran a line up here."

It was on the tip of my tongue to point out that the second floor was part of my house and *not* part of the lease agreement, but the fact was we all spent a lot of time up here.

That, and hey, free cable.

I turned as the news report came back on.

"Mystic's End mayor Mirabelle Saunders sends a message to citizens and visitors: Even though it's the joyful holiday season, people should take care to remember that too many holiday spirits can turn a great party into a destructive one," Kemp Henry, the single news anchor, told his audience. The broadcast cut to a pretty, middle-aged woman I didn't recognize, who cheerfully complimented Mystic's End for being particularly festive this year —even if, sometimes, situations may have got out of hand.

"This is more than two or three people," I told Gabe.

"It *must* be bad to get ol' maladroit Mirabelle out of her cave and onto the news," Ollie commented as he gazed at the mayor. "She doesn't show her face for much."

"Did you just call the mayor *maladroit?*" I asked chuckling.

"Yep. She really *is* just incompetent," Ollie said, nodding. "Mala-belle is her official behind-the-back nickname, and I think it's because anyone that whips out a check turns her into a malleable mayor that will agree with whatever it is money can buy in this town. Which, as you've seen, can be a lot." He frowned. "Anyway, I personally like the word maladroit. People don't use that word enough."

"You're so smart, honey," Pepper cooed and gave him a big, loud kiss.

Before I could roll my eyes again, I grabbed the remote and muted the volume as Mirabelle Saunders continued to cheerfully chastise the overenthusiastic revelers in Mystic's End. "Okay,

Ollie, let's get down to brass tacks. What could cause a mass number of people to suddenly get happy? Something in the water? In the air?"

"I've never seen or heard of anything like this. I mean, there's been some things here and there that seem to have statistical effects on people's happiness, like micrograms of lithium in drinking water lowering suicide rates, but this?" Ollie said, hitching his head toward Pepper. "Nothing like this."

"It's almost like she's on Ecstasy." Gabe moved toward us and looked at Pepper. "Really happy, really confident, no anxiety, increased emotionality."

I raised an eyebrow.

"I was a cop, remember? They have a dance club at the track."

Right.

And I couldn't see Gabe dancing, one with the world, at a rave, anyway.

"Yeah, but there are side effects to X, and she doesn't have them. Her blood pressure is fine, she's not extra thirsty. I mean, I could run her blood. That's probably the quickest way to figure out if she's been drugged." Ollie shifted to look at Gabe. "Thing is, X lasts only a few hours. She's been like this all day."

"A couple of days, really," I disagreed.

"She was fine on Thanksgiving," Gabe said.

"Yeah, but *was* she, though? All that bubblingly happy stuff about the parade?"

"Yeah, no, that was pretty normal. Okay, let's think. When was the first time Pepper started acting really out of character?"

"I'm *telling* you, it was Friday morning, and it was right after she went across the street to visit the new coffee shop," I insisted, pointing toward the window overlooking the square. "She came by here and visited with me before she went over to do her interview. She came back here and started acting a little strange. She didn't even do the interview properly. It got worse over the day."

"She was normal when she saw you that morning? You're sure?" Ollie asked me.

"Reasonably sure, yes." I nodded. "She wasn't here very long, but she seemed normal."

"Then that's where we start," Gabe said, looking down at Ollie. "You can stay here and watch her?"

"Yep. Get me a coffee, and I'll test it."

"Will do."

* * *

"We should have asked her what kind of coffee she got," Gabe muttered, and then blew on his hands as we walked across the square. The lights sparkled against the dark night sky and people clustered in small groups staring at the large tree in front of the old courthouse.

"It was a Macchiato. I saw it written on the cup when she handed it to me."

"I thought they weren't open Friday?"

"It looked like they weren't, but I didn't go over there. Maybe it was a soft opening or something. I saw them pull in furniture, but no big coffee machines. It's possible everything was already set up."

As we crossed the street in front of *The Golden Cup Coffee House*, we saw Chief Clutterbuck turning the corner and heading in the same direction we were. All three of us realized we were headed for the same door.

"Well, Wilcox, I know that you don't drink coffee after four because it upsets your delicate system," Clutterbuck drawled as he looked down at his former employee. He stood in front of the door—leaving us no choice but to talk to him. "So my guess is the two of you are here to look into why half the town is suddenly happy as a hog in mud. Am I right?"

Gabe shifted uncomfortably and rubbed his hands together again, blowing on them to warm them. Our cold breath fogged the air between us, and I shivered. "Chief, I'm sure they have other things in there besides coffee."

Clutterbuck's eyes narrowed. "Now, look here, Wilcox. I can't very well assign a detective to go and find out why the townsfolk are all suddenly happy. And we've been telling people that all day when they come into the station to report their loved ones are acting like kids let loose in an amusement park."

"That must be very difficult for you," Gabe told his former boss coldly. As he stared across the sidewalk at Clutterbuck, tension crackled between the two men. "To not be able to look into something you think could be wrong."

"What do you know, Wilcox? Tell me!" the chief demanded.

"I know I'd like to get into that coffee shop, sir," Gabe answered. "And you're blocking my way."

Frustration exploded from the chief, but I could feel that something else—something more substantial—was woven within it. I probed and pushed, trying to read what it was.

My cyes widened.

Fear.

Fear and...worry for someone he cared about a great deal. Someone he didn't know how to help.

Chief Clutterbuck wasn't angry.

Chief Clutterbuck was afraid.

"You know someone affected, don't you?" I asked him softly.

His gaze moved his eyes surprised. After a pause, he nodded.

"It's your daughter, isn't it? Evangeline has been struck by whatever this thing is."

"My daughter *hates* Christmas," Chief Clutterbuck told me, the words tumbling out of his mouth. It was as if he momentarily forgot his suspicion of me, forgot his firing of Gabe. Forgot that he wasn't supposed to trust us or be helpful to us. His arrogant mask fell away until he was just a father worried about his daughter and helpless to understand what he should do next. "Her mother died in a car accident on Christmas Day. Ever since then, she always hated the holidays."

Before he could continue, I was shocked that yet another mother and wife from Mystic's End was killed in an accident. I had looked up the numbers once—average accidental deaths per 100,000 people for unintentional injury deaths? Only 52.5. Just .05% of the population. Counting Mrs. Clutterbuck, Gabe's mother, Ollie's mother, it was...

Well, okay, just .07%.

Still, higher. And this was just among people I knew.

Gabe persisted in his refusal. "Look, I'm sorry

Evangeline is going through this, but we're not going to work with—"

"Gabe," I interrupted and placed a hand on his arm. "Chief Clutterbuck is right. You said yourself, as a private detective, you can't do anything about anything we find." I glanced at the head of the police department. "He can."

"We can't trust him," the detective objected.

"I can't trust you, either," Clutterbuck responded grimly, his eyes casting back and forth between us. "You both know you've been hiding things from me, and if you think *I* don't know it, you're underestimating me. I'm not going to ask you what. You keep your secrets, and I'll keep mine. But I've been dealing with this situation two days," Clutterbuck said, almost pleading. "We tested the water in the reservoir, the air. I traced Evangeline's steps. If this coffee shop doesn't pan out, I've hit a wall."

"Not hard enough, if you ask me," Gabe murmured.

Clutterbuck glared.

"We will if you answer one question. Why us?" I asked him. "Why have you come to us with this and not someone else? You could contact the governor, the sheriff. Heck, you could call the FBI into town, and they could dig into this place from top to bottom. Why do you want our help?"

"I suspect you know damn well why I can't call the FBI," Clutterbuck answered gruffly. I didn't answer, and after a pause, he went on. "Same for the sheriff and the governor. This is Mystic's End. We solve our own problems. We don't involve outsiders."

"That's an answer regarding why you won't call them. That doesn't tell me why you want us."

"Because I do," he answered, and did not elaborate. After a pause: "Can you just accept that?"

Gabe shook his head no before he had any time to think it over.

"Gabe, you *have* worked with him before."

"Yeah, I know," he told me. Staring Clutterbuck in the eyes, his chest puffed out, he added, "That's the problem."

An angry chief of police turned on his heel and stormed inside.

* * *

The smell of coffee hit me as soon as we entered the warm space. Maybe a dozen residents were seated at trendy wrought-iron tables in twos and fours sipping various cups and glasses of frothy or bubbling beverages.

An extended counter ran almost the entire

length of the right side of the shop, stacked with chrome espresso and frothing machines, bean grinders, and bottles of coffee flavorings. A glass case holding a sparse selection of muffins, cookies, and pastries sat near the back next to a cash register.

"Hello there!" a college-age girl with a nose-ring called over the counter. "Are the three of you together?"

"No!" Clutterbuck and Gabe barked out simultaneously.

I telepathically probed the barista to see if there was anything odd about her. She had the distinct feel of a human, memories and thoughts that any ordinary early twenty-something would have. Nothing emotionally out of place about her. She was happy without being exuberant, friendly without being over the top.

"Did you guys just open up?" I asked pleasantly.

"We did!" she smiled, nodding so vigorously her ponytail bounced. "Just this weekend. I thought I was going to have to try and get a job at the track or something"—the girl frowned and made a sour face —"but I was just visiting the square on Friday with my family, and this place was hiring! Isn't that lucky?"

"Jewel!" Dalida Dodd snapped from the back. "Ask them what they want, please." The elegant

Dalida walked from the end of the counter toward the young employee as the girl's face fell. "What did I tell you about the chit chat? People want their coffee, and they want to move along."

"Yes, Miss Dodd. Sorry, Miss Dodd," Jewel nodded. Turning toward us, she asked what she could get us. "I'd like an iced coffee, please. And a macchiato to go." I could spot there were precisely three types of coffees available, and I had just covered two types.

"A light roast black, to go," Gabe added. And that covered all three.

Jewel nodded quickly and scurried off to prepare the drinks.

"Chief Clutterbuck." Dalida smiled widely and reached her hand across the counter. "It's nice to meet you. I'm Dalida Dodd. I'd been told you might stop by this weekend."

"Oh? By who?" he asked as he shook her hand.

"Please, let me know what you would like, and I'd be happy to prepare it for you myself. On the house," the proprietor smiled warmly without answering his question. "A cappuccino? Café au lait, perhaps?"

There were at least three employees behind the counter. Two were working and one seemed to have nothing in particular to do. My eyes narrowed at Dalida's offer to prepare the chief's coffee herself. I watched her like a hawk as she grabbed a cup with the golden logo on it and waited for his answer.

"Um, just a coffee, ma'am. Thank you."

Dalida Dodd walked casually to the back and poured a cup of coffee from a carafe at the end of the counter. "Cream or sugar?" she called back.

"No, ma'am, just black," he answered.

I watched her hands intently, but I could see nothing suspicious in her handling of the coffee. She slipped nothing in the coffee. Except...except there were only three coffees on offer this late at night, and Gabe and I had ordered all three.

Jewel never came within five feet of Dalida's special carafe.

"Here you go," the woman said, handing the cup over the counter. "On the house, Chief. That goes for you and any of your men." Jewel came up simultaneously and handed Gabe and me our order.

"Let's go," I whispered to the two.

Gabe frowned. "Don't you want to talk to—"

"Let's go," I whispered again more insistently. Gabe nodded, grabbed the coffee, and moved toward the door. Chief Clutterbuck, looking confused, followed him.

I thanked Jewel and glanced once last time at Dalida Dodd—who stared at me, an odd amusement in her eyes as I left her coffee shop.

"Don't drink any of that," I told the two men who waited outside for me. "She gave him a drink from a coffee pot that we didn't get coffee from. We need to get it to Ollie and test it."

Gabe held his hand out.

Clutterbuck stared back at him.

Gabe frowned. "You're not going to just give us that coffee so we can test it, are you?"

Clutterbuck smiled wide. "Nope." Turning he said, "Your place, I assume?" and without waiting for an answer set off across the square clutching his coffee cup tightly.

SEVEN

"The Chief of Police is here!" Pepper said excitedly as Clutterbuck stepped onto the second floor living area. "Terry, baby, how're you doin'?" The carefree reporter pushed herself up off the couch with all the elation of a sports fan who just witnessed the game-winning touchdown, and rushed the head of MEPD. "You're looking pouty, Terry. Why are you so pouty?"

I blinked. Terry?

Ollie gently pulled Pepper off the older man with murmured apologies.

"Well, now I know why you two are involved in this mess," Terrance Clutterbuck gruffed, and set the coffee down on the dining table. "You three, I suppose," he added, looking Ollie up and down.

"No rule says I can't check into things I'm curious about on my own," Ollie responded, leading Pepper back to the couch. Gideon sat just beyond them, staring at the police chief suspiciously.

"I'm actually on a case," Gabe told his old boss. "The Bellingers. Joe came to see me. It appears Harriet has gotten happy the last couple of days, and he's a bit out of sorts about it. Hired me to find out what happened to her."

Chief Clutterbuck dropped his eyes, sighed, and nodded. "Yeah, I can see that." Raising his gaze, he shrugged. "He came to us to report it, but there's not much we can do. Harriet insists she's fine. *Everyone* who's suddenly got the giggles claims they're just fine, and they don't want to answer questions. Until they break the law, there's nothing we can do about it."

I found that hard to believe.

Even though I encouraged Gabe Wilcox to accept Clutterbuck's help, I was still unnerved at having the man in my home. When Claire's greyhound, Petey, ran away, Clutterbuck swooped in and had Azalea arrested for the crime before there was any evidence to suggest one had taken place. When I confronted him, he was *offensively* rude.

And that wasn't the first time the chief and I had tangoed. This wasn't even the first time he'd been in my house—before I was open two months, he was in here with a search warrant.

Let's face it. Chief Terrance Clutterbuck had suspected me of having a hand in every crime I was tangentially connected to. If there was no crime, he found a way to arrest someone for something.

Jeeves had said Clutterbuck changed his mind about me. Thought I could be useful to him.

I wasn't sure I wanted to be useful to a man like that.

"What about the party the mayor was talking about on the news?" Gabe asked, nodding toward the television. "It seems there were some crimes committed there."

"It was piddly misdemeanor stuff," the head cop answered gruffly. "Nothing Mirabelle needed to crawl out of her mansion to deal with if you ask me. They'd all scattered by the time we showed up. Other than the host, we don't even know who was there."

"Have you talked to Mayor Saunders about the situation?" I asked.

The man nodded once. "Mayor Saunders is a member of the Holy Grove Church, and the only reason she cares one whit about a bunch of people having a good time, spending money like it grows on trees and raising tax revenue for the town is that

Reverend Kane's off his rocker with the rest of them." The chief looked at Ollie. "Sorry, son."

"My dad's afflicted with whatever this is?" Ollie asked, frowning at Clutterbuck in disbelief.

"Wouldn't have thought it," Clutterbuck nodded. "Always thought he was protected from things like this. You know what I mean, son?"

Ollie shifted uncomfortably.

"What does that mean?" I asked between the chief and Ollie. Ollie looked away.

I turned, and Clutterbuck stared at me with uncomfortable intensity. For a moment, I thought I would get an answer—but then he shrugged and didn't respond.

Gabe and I stared at each other, eyebrows raised.

"Ollie, are you going to test those coffees?" Clutterbuck asked, turning. "If so, you better get on that. I don't want to hang out here and do nothing any longer than I have to."

"Can you?" Ollie asked me, gesturing toward Pepper. I nodded. "Okay, who's coming to the lab with me? I'll run an unknown substance test since I have that equipment. It'll take a few hours. If we get anything we can't figure out, we may have to send it to the state."

"Let's try and avoid that," Clutterbuck told him.

"I'll come with you," Gabe added. "It's already

pretty late. How about we meet back here in the morning?" He caught my eye and winked, and a loud I WILL FIND OUT WHAT THAT WAS ABOUT screamed in my head.

I winced.

Clutterbuck and Gabe followed Ollie down the stairs.

* * *

M iss Bessie shimmered into view. "Thought you could use some help with Giggles over there."

Pepper squealed and bounced around the room, talking excitedly about the holiday season. "We have to have dinner at *the Club*—oh, I know you hate Evangeline, but I think she might be nice under all that mean, you know? Oh oh oh, we have to go to the casino. You've never even *been* to the casino, have you? No, I'm sure you haven't," she jabbered at a hundred miles an hour.

I grabbed the remote and clicked the television on.

"Television!" she screeched and flew across the room. She landed on the couch with such force it slid across the room and thumped loudly against the wall. "Oh! I love this show!"

"Unless you can make her go to sleep, I'm not sure how much help you'll be," I told the ghost.

"Well, I flew around town to see what I could see," Miss Bessie told me as we watched Pepper laugh uproariously at a sitcom that had never been quite *that* funny. "The holiday season is in full swing, so it's hard to spot people that are having a better time than they would normally have unless I know 'em. What I *can* tell you is that the old folks home?" She raised her eyebrow. "It's like a bacchanal up there."

I blinked. "The whole place? Like, everybody?"

"Josie was dancing on a table when I got there, shakin' her hips like there was a light or two burned out on her string. Harold Whatnow was throwing dollar bills at her feet while she clopped around in those ugly orthopedic shoes just as crazy as a bullbat—and *that* man? That man would squeeze a nickel 'til the buffalo screamed," Miss Bessie said, crossing her arms. "Harold doesn't throw money at *anything* other than a mutual fund."

Mystic Memories Senior Living Center's residents might have gone on a field trip to the town square for the holidays and got coffee—but I didn't remember seeing them. It wasn't possible, though, that they would have done so without stopping by my store. My students always came in to visit and get supplies when they came into town.

I sighed, thinking. Then asked, "What about the staff?"

"Pouring the margaritas. I'm telling you, Fortuna, the whole place's gone nuts."

I thought for another minute. "Can you do me a favor?" I asked.

"Sure, what is it?"

"Can you go back up there and look at the activity schedule behind the front desk? Tell me what was scheduled for the past few days. Did they go anywhere in particular, did anyone special come in?"

"Well, of course, people came *in*, Fortuna," Bessie frowned pointedly at me. "Thanksgiving was just a few days ago. There was a big dinner with guests, food ordered from a restaurant—"

"What restaurant?" I interrupted.

"Well, I don't *know*, dear, I wasn't invited," Miss Bessie scowled, her tone like that of a spoiled child. "I'm dead, you see, and since I'm dead, I don't get invited to the good parties anymore. Clearly." She leaned back, her eyebrows pinched low. "Everything fun happens now that I'm dead. That's just unfair."

"Miss Bessie, you have no idea whether those people are in control of themselves, whether they're drugged, if they might have long-term damage. Don't get upset you missed a party. Be grateful you had moved on before you got caught up in this. No one's been hurt...yet," I said, glancing at Pepper jumping up and down on my coffee table. "I'm not sure that will hold if this spreads. Or gets worse."

Miss Bessie looked at me with hard-eyed suspicion. "You don't like happy people, do you, dear? You always have that sour puss on your face about something."

I stared at the ghost with what I hoped was unnerving directness.

"Oh, crack a smile once in a while, Fortuna. Your face won't break," Miss Bessie said as she floated up. "Anything else you want me to try and find out while I'm there? And if I find out what happy juice everyone is drinking, you want me to bring you a shot of it so you can loosen up?"

Without waiting for an answer, Miss Bessie shimmered and disappeared.

* * *

An hour later, Pepper and I were watching a re-run of Lassie. As sorrowful music played and a woman wept over a lost dog, my friend smiled and bounced happily while remarking about how amazing the woman's makeup was holding up.

Before I could answer, Jeeves climbed in the window silently and surveyed the room with a complete lack of self-consciousness. He looked flushed—I hope that meant he traveled here quickly and not that the vampire just slurped up a jovial Mystic's End citizen.

"Holy cow! Can you fly?" Pepper asked him excitedly, launching herself off the sofa. "Oh, man, come on—take me flying!"

"There's a door, you know." I pointed toward the stairs.

"I can't stay long." The vampire ignored Pepper, walking around her until he was in front of me. Jeeves extended a hand to help me up.

I stared at it. "Where are we going?"

Jeeves glanced at Pepper as she sat back down, enraptured by the show again. "Out of earshot."

"I can't," I said, waving his hand away. "Something's going on with Pepper. Hell, the whole town, actually. I can't leave her alone right now."

He glanced at her. "Let me guess. She's quite happy?"

"That would be the understatement of the year." I gestured for him to sit down, and after a short pause, he did. "According to Miss Bessie, the whole senior home is infected with whatever this is. Pepper's got it. Dexter Kane. Gabe's got a case he's working on where a husband is trying to find out why his normally bitter wife is now in such a great mood."

"Yes, yes, we see the same thing up at the track —but I'm not here about that," Jeeves said, and a cold tremor ran through my body as I guessed what he was here for. "You used magic, didn't you?"

"Look, Jeeves, it was just to unlock a door. It was automatic," I said, somewhat defensively.

"*Damn* it, Fortuna," the vampire muttered, putting his hands over his face. "Why can't you just do what you're asked to do?"

I frowned. Suddenly, Jeeves sounded an awful lot like the oh-so-controlling Martin Salvi, and I wasn't in the mood to add another well-meaning but overly protective jerk to the repertoire.

If he even *was* well-meaning.

Which to be honest, I still didn't know.

"Because I'm my own person, and I make my own decisions, Jeeves. *You* don't make them for me," I told him fiercely. I thought about letting him have it, but got myself calmed down pretty quickly. I reminded myself I did tell him I would not do magic —and I broke my word. "Look, I'm sorry. To tell you the truth, I wasn't thinking. I tend to be pretty laser-focused on one thing at a time, and I was worried about Pepper. Marty Salvatore's visit just faded from my mind."

"Ooh, let's watch a mob movie!" Pepper said, shaking my shoulder. "Let's watch *The Godfather*, Fortuna! Or *Goodfellas*!"

I pushed Pepper's hand away and changed the channel, grateful for Gabe installing cable with its hundreds of channels.

"Music videos!" she shouted and jumped up to dance.

Jeeves sat quietly, a faraway look in his dark eyes, and I frowned. That look signaled a telepathic communication with Martin, but I could hear nothing. Martin must not be close. A peculiar expression flashed across his face, and then he nodded.

"Jeeves? Are you here for something, or just to give me guff for my mistake?"

The vampire turned and reached into a small duffel bag he brought with him. "I have something for you." Gently, very gently, he pulled out three witch bottles, the bottles that Martin's aunt had found, and set them carefully on the coffee table. "Aunt Addie asked that I get these to you, and Martin agreed. She's afraid that one of Don Salvatore's witches could find them, and she doesn't want anything to happen to them."

I stared at the hundred-plus-year-old bottles in bewildered incomprehension. They sparkled as if they were alive.

Which, technically, they might be.

Both Martin and Miss Bessie believed these bottles held the souls of the descendants of the

Delphi Coven. Women that eventually defied the town's men in power and who, one by one, died accidentally, young, and tragically—only to be captured in a witch bottle by the town's curse.

A curse I didn't know if I believed existed.

A story I didn't know if I believed was true.

But Martin and Jeeves did, and I was shocked they would hand them over.

"Why me?" I asked him quietly. "If the Dreamboat Don is here to discover if I exist and I just did magic exposing myself, is this place *really* the safest place for them?"

"We are playing a dangerous game, Fortuna." Jeeves stood up. "If something happens to us, Martin wanted to be sure that the bottles were safe." He paused. "Look. We made the choices we made in life, and we accepted the consequences for those choices. Those women, whoever they may be," Jeeves pointed, "they did not. They should not suffer for our mistakes."

"How am *I* supposed to protect them? And what mistakes?" I asked him, standing up.

"You are the mystic," Jeeves whispered as he leaned forward, his eyes meeting mine with a mixture of mournfulness and affection. "You will know what to do. You have to protect them the same way I must protect Martin. You will do your duty." He gave me a half-smile. "I must return to mine."

"But—"

"I must go." Jeeves moved back swiftly, and within a blink, he was halfway out the window.

"Jeeves, damn it, tell me what the hell is going on!" I shouted after him.

"Ooh, vampire, you in trouble now," Pepper sing-songed as she shook her finger at Jeeves.

"Take care of them," Jeeves repeated.

And then he was gone.

EIGHT

"Ooh, pretty!" Pepper cooed, snatching up an old blue bottle. She held it up to the light, and it seemed to flash with brilliance.

"Pepper, no. Give that back," I told her, clasping the bottom of the smooth glass.

"Hey! Cut it out!" Pepper yanked the top of the bottle clumsily, smiling. "I wanna see!"

"Pepper, I'm serious," I warned, my voice rising slightly. "Let it go."

"Nuh-uh." She gripped tighter while balancing her weight, flexing her knees as if testing her own stability.

"Pepper!"

Pepper's grin grew wider. She slowly gave a tug,

and then another, trying to wrest the bottle from my hand. "I want to see it. Gimme."

"Do you *remember* what these are?" I flung forward as Pepper yanked. "Be careful with it! You don't know what would happen if you drop—"

"I don't care what they are, Tuna-face." Pepper's eyebrows furrowed and she tightened her grip and gave a great yank. I held tight. She yanked again. We stood across from each other in a struggle for control of the witch bottle. "I wanna see it!"

Everything seemed slow motion, the bottle going back and forth between us as we locked in an epic tug-of-war. The television blared in the background, now ignored. Pushing and pulling against one another, we banged against chairs, tables, and the couch. What started as mild annoyance on my part was quickly giving way to panic as my feet slid against the floor, unable to find traction.

"Pepper, the bottle's going to break! Let it go!"

But she didn't let it go.

What she did do was grab the top of the bottle and give a final yank—and flew back against the wall as the bottle un-stoppered with a loud pop.

"No! I wanted *that* part, not *this* part," she said, holding up the cork. "This part isn't pretty!"

The bottle glowed.

A roar built in the room punctuated by the

sizzle and crack of energy so powerful my hair stood up on my arms. Within seconds, shimmery gold fog seeped from the bottle's mouth. It spilled slowly, ever so gradually, to the floor and built up in the room like a fog. Gideon looked curiously at it.

"Ooh, pretty," Pepper breathed, her eyes wide.

"Oh, Pepper, what have you done," I whispered, too shocked to move.

The light bulbs in the room flashed, then dimmed, then blinked again.

I determined early on that I would *not* open these bottles without getting a lot more explanation as to what they held, and what the consequences would be of opening them.

But I hadn't done any of those things.

My methodical (okay, procrastinating) approach meant I was woefully unprepared for the supernatural smoke pouring into my living room at a slow, but steady, pace.

I tensed, waiting.

The bottle's glow was dimming, and the cascade of beclouded sparkle pouring from it devolved to just a trickle. Like fog from a machine at a disco, it spread out on the floor in all directions curling around our ankles.

Then, suddenly, it froze, flashed, and spiraled in a whirlpool in front of me.

"Pepper, get behind me," I whispered, yanking her.

"But now I can't see!"

The whirling tornado stretched upward, I watched as the lightning flashed through the transparent whirlwind. Tiny contained strikes that sounded like little thundering cracks lit up the room. I shuddered as the air grew cooler, then cold, despite the fury of electrical activity taking place. The circling fog slowed, flashed outward once more, and then coalesced rapidly to form the image of a woman.

Then the glow faded from the bottle, and all was quiet.

"Who are you?" I demanded.

But before she could answer, I gasped.

Gabe's eyes stared back at me.

"You're Mary, Gabe's mother," I guessed. "Miss Bessie's daughter."

"I am," she nodded, tilting her head. "And one of you must be the current mystic."

* * *

"Ooh! I love this show!" Pepper shouted as she looked around for something to entertain her now that she could no longer see the spectral guest that had just arrived. "Fortuna, look! The show with the horses!" *Gunsmoke* was playing.

"So, *she's* not the mystic," I pointed out.

"How do you know my mother and son?" Mary asked, stretching her arms above her.

I was always amazed at how ghosts relied on actions that had comforted them when they were alive, but that held no real meaning now that they were dead. Mary had no muscles, so there was nothing to stretch. Yet she perceived that her actions stretched muscles long gone from her control.

"Gabe is—was—a detective. He came to check me out when I first moved here," I answered as if I conversed with a ghost every day. Which I did, technically. Just not *this* ghost. "Miss Bessie sought me out when I moved here because I am a descendant of the Delphi Coven."

"Oh? Whose daughter are you?" Mary asked with interest.

"I don't know."

The ghost blinked. "You don't know?"

"I was adopted by a family in California. I moved to this town in the hopes that I could find out where I came from," I said, spilling the truths to the ghost with ease that I had spent months hiding from everyone else. "When I got here, Miss Bessie made me the mystic, and...well, things got complicated."

"I imagine so," she smiled warmly. "I was prepared to become the mystic, and yet I wasn't really looking forward to it, if you want to know the truth." Her long, butter-colored hair grew full before my eyes as she slowly solidified the image of herself in her own mind. "You must have enormous power," Mary smiled again. "Thank you for freeing me."

"I...I, um, didn't, actually," I said, shifting uncomfortably. "Well, not intentionally. Pepper and I were fighting over the bottle, and it opened. I hadn't intended to let you out."

Mary stared at me, the smile fading from her face. "I'm surprised you admitted that."

"That's not what I mean," I said, suddenly realizing how that sounded. "Look, ma'am, if the stories were *true*, I *would* have been happy to let you out." Her sudden appearance, coupled with chaos of the happy-go-lucky pandemic, rattled me. "I had no way to know for sure they were true, and I didn't know what I would unleash on this town if I opened those bottles. So I waited."

"So polite and careful not to give offense," Mary observed wryly. "You must not have obtained the book yet."

"The magic book with the blank pages? Leather-bound?" I asked.

Mary nodded.

"No, I found it."

Mary blinked. "Did Anne Sperling not tell you through the book what you needed to do?"

"Who's Anne Sperling?" I asked, confused. When Mary didn't answer, I continued. "I don't know who that is, but all the book really told me to do was learn how to scry."

"And did you?"

Miss Bessie shimmered into view, already on a roll. "So, they went to the casino on Tuesday," she announced with a shrug. "I don't understand why they like that place. Just a big black hole for your money, if you ask me. Of course, no one ever does," the old woman announced as she turned to check on Pepper—

—and stopped, staring at Mary, her eyes wide.

"Mary," Miss Bessie whispered, her voice choking with emotion. "My girl...my baby girl... you're here!"

"Oh, no. No, Mama...you're dead," Mary whispered back, heartbroken.

If ghosts could look unsteady, the two women looked unsteady. Arms lifted, fingers reached toward one another, and sobs escaped from tight lips while Pepper, oblivious, cheered on the calvary.

I drew back to give the two women room for their reunion.

"I am, but don't you worry. It was just in time, too," Miss Bessie said, closing the distance between them. "If I hadn't been when we found you, I would have thrown myself off a cliff just to see your beautiful face again." Their arms outstretched, they embraced one another.

Which, to be honest, shocked the heck out of me. Since they're made of energy, I didn't think they could, you know, hug. But hug they did.

"How did you release Mary, Fortuna?" Miss Bessie asked after several minutes. "How did you know which bottle she was in?"

"She didn't," Mary told her mother, her steely gaze lingering on me for no more than a moment before she turned back to her mother. "According to her, it was an accident. The mystic had no intention of releasing the coven from the bottles. I just got lucky when she and her friend began fighting over my prison."

My relationship with Gabe's mother was not getting off to a great start.

It seemed like none of my relationships in this town started off well.

"Now, that's not exactly what I said. I said I didn't know—"

"You know now," Mary snapped, cutting me off. She pointed at the other two bottles.

"Mary, I know you don't know Fortuna," Miss Bessie told her daughter gently, but Mary held up a hand to silence her mother. The old woman's gentle tone turned to granite in an instant. "Young lady, don't you give me the hand!" Miss Bessie snapped back. "You've been locked in a bottle for damn near thirty years! Unless you have a radio in that thing, you don't know anything about anything!"

Mary inclined her head once and lowered her hand slowly—but never dropped her stare.

"My stars, your defiance hasn't mellowed at all, has it?" Miss Bessie glared at her daughter.

"Did you think it would after you *refused* to hand over the mystic title?" Mary asked her, crossing her arms. "Whose fault was it that I couldn't protect myself when I needed to?"

"Whose fault was it that you decided to date a townsman descendant?" Miss Bessie snapped back. "Of all the stupid things you did, Mary—and boy, did you do a lot of stupid things—that *had* to be the stupidest! How did you *think* that relationship was going to turn out?"

"Not with me ten feet underwater, Mother, that's for sure!" Mary exploded.

Pepper looked at her phone and frowned at it. "My phone's going haywire," she complained, holding it out to me. "The words in the app aren't making any sense."

I grabbed the phone and looked.

STARS. DEFY. HAS. FAULT. REFUSE. PROTECT. STUPID.

Miss Bessie and Mary's words were being flung so fast and furious the *Ghosts, Ghosts Everywhere* app that enabled communication from the great beyond was struggling to keep up.

"We have a new ghost that stopped by," I told her quietly. "It will likely take the sensors some time to tune in to what she's saying."

"Really? Cool. Ooh! Chia! I'm going to watch the show," Pepper said, turning back to the television. An infomercial outlined the incredible benefits of owning a chia-sprouting terra cotta figurine that looked like the president. Pepper dialed in to the number to order one.

"How long did *you* know about those three bottles?" Mary shouted at her mother.

"Don't talk to me like that, young lady! I've done the best I could!"

"Yeah, well," Mary rolled her eyes and waved her hands up and down to show off her simmering spectral image. "Clearly *not* great, Mom."

"You know, I felt *far* more affection for you before you got out of that bottle, opened your mouth and started talking," Miss Bessie told her daughter. "Maybe we should go back to that."

Mary gasped. "Mother!"

"What's going on?" Gabe asked, smiling as he stepped onto the second floor. "Pepper okay?"

I looked at Mary and Miss Bessie, who'd both frozen to stare at Gabe.

"Hey, um...maybe you should come sit down," I moved forward and pulled the earbud out of Gabe's ear so Miss Bessie and Mary's fighting (should it start again) wouldn't reach him.

* * *

"She's here?" Gabe asked, swallowing. "My mother is here?"

I nodded.

Both women watched Gabe silently absorb the description of what took place while he was off investigating the happy-demic. Toward the middle of the story, he reached out and clutched my hand. The gesture brought a smile to Miss Bessie's face...

...and a frown to Mary's.

His face was etched in shock. I told the story slowly, pausing periodically so Gabe could ask any questions he had. But he had none. He simply looked at me for long moments, his facial muscles twitching and tensing, and then nodded for me to go on.

Once I was through, he didn't seem to know what to do with himself.

"Tell him to put in the earbud so I can talk to him," Miss Bessie demanded.

"No," I told her quietly. "Let him process this. Just be patient."

Gabe swallowed. "Are you talking to her right now?"

I shook my head, no. "Miss Bessie wants to talk to you."

I was flooded by fear, and I realized it was coming from Gabe. Not Gabe, the man, but Gabe, the little boy who never got to say goodbye to his mother. Who never understood why she went away. And who wasn't sure, despite everything he'd seen since I moved to town, he really believed that his mother, lost so long ago, was now back and standing just three feet from him.

"Can she hear me?"

I nodded. "Of course. If you have something to say, just say it."

He closed his eyes, and tears leaked out and made a pathway down his flushed cheeks. Gideon got up and sauntered over to the detective so he could lay his head down across his lap. The greyhound pushed his head against Gabe's chest as if to reassure him he wasn't alone. The detective reached for him.

"I love you, Mother," Gabe whispered without opening his eyes. "But I need...I need some time. You, too, Gram. I just...I need some time."

"What is with everyone needing *time?*" Miss Bessie asked with exasperation.

"Those women locked in those bottles request that you not take too much time," Mary said with resentment in her low voice. She stared not at me, but at the two bottles sitting on the table. "Locked in a glass purgatory, deaf and blind to the world around you?" Mary shuddered. "It's a hell I wouldn't wish upon anyone."

Gabe pulled away and turned his back. "I just need a little time," he repeated as if he heard his mother's complaint.

"Gabe's processing isn't about them," I told Mary. "It's about you. I'll let them out," I said, her face lighting up with excitement. "But you're going to have to wait a little while. Something's going on with the townspeople, and before anyone gets hurt, we need to figure out what it is."

"Mystic, it will take you just minutes to—"

"My name is Fortuna—I'm a person, not a title —and I told you how it's going to be," I said, cutting Gabe's mother off. "I don't know what's going on yet, and I don't want to juggle two crises at once."

Plus I had no idea what the consequences would be of letting Gabe's mother out. If it was magic, did Martin's father sense it? Did his witch brigade know what happened?

"There's *always* a crisis," Miss Bessie murmured.

"Right now, you're expecting more of me than you expected of yourselves," I told her harshly. "You never found any bottles"—I pointed at Miss Bessie, and then raised an eyebrow at Mary—"and you couldn't keep yourself safe. I may not be doing things the way you want them done, but I'm making progress, and I'm still alive. Right now, the witch bottles are safe. Pepper's not. I might not be. So back off."

Mary glared at me.

Like I said. Not starting off well.

NINE

"Why does that woman look like a peppermint candy?" Mary asked us the next morning as Pepper sat at the table eating sugary donuts for breakfast. The reporter giggled like a child and showed me the red and green sprinkles on her fingertips, then licked them off excitedly. "Is that hairstyle common now?"

"No. Well—so, those artificial colors are more common now than when you were alive." Miss Bessie floated over to Pepper, looked down, and frowned. "Before you died, only punks dyed their hair those colors. Now, everyone and their dog does it."

Gideon jerked his head up and turned with big, panicked eyes.

"Calm down, dog. No one's dyeing your hair red and white. Your skin is much too delicate to tolerate hair dye, so relax," I told him, placing a bowl of homemade dog food in front of the greyhound. I was trying to encourage him to eat healthier and lay off the bacon. Gideon's eyes narrowed as he stared at the brown rice, ground turkey, spinach, peas, carrots, and zucchini. I couldn't cook much, but I figured dog food might be an excellent place to start. "Just try it, Gid," I told him as I scratched his ears.

Gideon leaned forward and sniffed. Then he pulled his head back up. The dog stared at the bowl of healthy food, his tail flat on the floor, ears down. He was the picture of misery.

"I could dye his hair. There are vegan, skin-safe, organic semi-permanent hair dyes now," Liz said as she hopped up the stairs. "You just let me know what color, and I'll get on that. He's pretty dark, though." Liz scratched his ears. "It would probably just be a color sheen."

Gideon yanked his head from her hand and scampered away. Spike floated in behind her, stopped, and stared at the two ghosts standing in his kitchen.

"Who the heck are you?" he blurted out rudely, gaping at Mary.

"Spike, that's Miss Bessie's daughter," I told him

as I opened the fridge and pulled out a bag of bacon bits I'd got at the store. Setting them on the counter, I grabbed Gideon's food bowl and sprinkled them on top. "Last night Jeeves brought three of the coven witch bottles Addie had. He wanted me to keep them safe. One got opened."

"Oh, man, seriously? Three more ghosts?" he said with exasperation. "You know, I'm the resident ghost of this place. I feel like I should be consulted before even more ghosts move in."

"I have not moved in, young man," Mary snapped at him.

"Oh, please, lady," Spike rolled his eyes. "She died"—Spike pointed an accusing finger at Miss Bessie—"and she's been here every day since then. Then her grandson moved in. Now you. What next? Any ghost pets we need to contact? Do we need to build out the place?"

"Spike, that's really rude," Liz said. "You're almost always over at my place, anyway. What do you care who hangs out at Fortuna's?"

"She's literally the only person in the whole town any ghost can talk to!" Spike whined at Liz.

"Hey, I may answer slowly so that the app can translate, but I talk to you." Liz told Spike, referencing the *Ghosts, Ghosts* app that picked up and passed on most of what the ghosts around us said to the non-paranormals.

"They're all going to live here! It's not right!" he responded hotly.

I sighed and stared at the carefully crafted bowl of dog food (now mixed heavily with thick bacon bits). I couldn't even get my greyhound to stop eating tons of bacon. How was I going to manage a gaggle of ghosts, a happy-demic, Gabe's reaction to his mother, Martin's father...

"Hey," Liz said, turning my head toward her with a fingertip. I met her eyes. "You okay?"

"Have you seen what's going on around here?" I asked her.

"Like, here in this house, or here in this town?"

"Yes."

"That's actually one of the reasons I came over. I was going to ask you about it before I caught the overwhelmed look on your face."

"I'm fine," I said, but I could hear my voice was raspy. "It's just a lot going on, you know? And I'm worried about everyone. Pepper"—I waved toward my friend bouncing happily in front of the television as Bugs Bunny ran from Porky Pig —"seems to be getting worse. And everyone's claiming that people are happy, but..." I stared at Pepper again, my brow furrowed. "It's more than that."

Liz frowned. "What do you mean?"

"It's like she's got no impulse control," I told the

hairdresser as I set the bacon-laced bowl down and snapped for Gideon. Suddenly, I leaned up, my eyes wide. "That's it. The people in the store yesterday, too. I don't think whatever's going on is about making people happy. I think it's making them impulsive."

Liz turned to look at Pepper, her eyes narrowing. "I'm not sure I'm following."

"Think about it. That crazy hair dye thing, her grabbing for anything she wants without regard to consequences, getting constantly distracted by something or another. It was the same with the people in the shop yesterday," I told her, my voice low. The look on Pepper's face, grabbing the bottle without a care for the consequences, flashed in my memory. "They bought or tried to buy everything in the shop that wasn't nailed down. Every painting went out of the door. Heck, one woman even tried to buy a sign."

Liz thought about what I said and nodded. "What could be causing it?"

"I don't know." I crossed my arms. "But this isn't, like, impaired impulse control. This is non-existent impulse control."

As Liz and I watched, Gideon trotted up to his bowl, sniffed again, and ate delicately from the carefully crafted bowl. The bowl scraped the floor and caught Pepper's attention.

She turned swiftly and yanked the bowl from the dog, scooping the food into her mouth with her fingers. Gideon, Liz, and I stared at her in amazement.

After a few moments of silent horror, Liz turned and said in a deadpan voice, "Yeah, okay, I'll buy non-existent impulse control."

* * *

I'd assumed that since it was Monday morning, most of the hordes that invaded Mystic's End over the Thanksgiving weekend would have been long gone. Once I went downstairs to open up my shop and looked out onto the street, that assumption was proven entirely wrong.

The streets were packed with disheveled people clutching fistfuls of cash. They moved from shop to shop, staring greedily through the windows. Cars tried to pick through the throng without running anyone over. That was no small feat as people shot out into the street without looking.

And that was just the people that took the sidewalks as a suggestion—many people didn't even bother with that.

"Okay, this is ridiculous already," I said out loud.

"Where are all these people coming from?"

Spike asked as he stared out the window.

"Out of town? Everyone took extra days off?" I guessed. "I don't know."

Avoiding my problems would not make them go away. Still, I honestly didn't know what to do without hearing from Ollie about the tests on the coffee.

I was also wondering if my initial guess at the cause of all this was incorrect.

The sheer number of people wandering around in the street, Jeeves's report that people at the track were acting crazy...I wondered whether this many people could have possibly had coffee at The Golden Cup. Anything slipped into a drink should have worn off by now, and Pepper hadn't been out of my place in over twenty-four hours.

I felt eyes on me. Looking across the square, I saw Dalida Dodd staring back at me.

What was it with that woman? Did she have a sixth sense?

I snickered to myself. That was kind of funny coming from me.

"Are you getting sick, too?" Spike asked, his voice filled with alarm.

"What? No, no, I'm fine," I assured him. My mood wasn't bright enough to be infected with the happy-demic, though I was feeling a little loopy from all the anxiety I was trying to keep at bay.

"Okay, just making sure. Hey, I, uh, wanted to come down here and apologize to you," Spike said without looking at me. "This place still feels like my house and stuff, and...well, I know it's not. I shouldn't have got all mad about the other ghost."

I waved a hand dismissively. "Don't worry about it."

"It was just really quiet for a long time, you know? And I was thrilled when you showed up, and it wasn't quiet anymore."

"I don't recall that." I recalled Spike being a poltergeist to scare me out of the place.

"Okay, maybe not at first," Spike rolls his eyes. "Then, I was."

"But?"

"But now it's never just you and me. It's never quiet," he smiled sheepishly. "I can go out to the woods and hang there, and it's quiet and peaceful and stuff, but I kinda miss when it was just us. Well, us and Gideon."

"Things are definitely changing," I murmured as I gazed out the window. I think I was talking more to myself than anyone else.

"Yeah, I spent a lot of time not changing."

"One thing hasn't changed, Spike."

"Yeah," he asked half-smiling. "What's that?"

"This is still your house."

He blinked. "Thanks, Fortuna."

"No problem."

Spike looked at the door. "Are we going to open?"

The sound of glass breaking outside drew my attention back to the window.

I peered out between the blinds, scanning the town center to find the source of the noise, realizing it was a liquor store on the west end of the square. Their storefront had been shattered, and excited tourists climbed excitedly through the gaping frame.

"Nope," I snapped, stepping back. "Move away from the window."

I pulled my hands up, palms against the window, and whispered the duplicating spell Gunther had taught me. With barely any notice, I double-paned and then triple-paned the glass. "There. That should be pretty much unbreakable."

"Won't they just break all three?" Spike asked, confused.

"It's a polycarbonate glass. Virtually unbreakable," I told him as I pulled down the hours sign and moved the closed sign to a more prominent position on the door. "Three panes should be even more unbreakable."

My cell phone rang. I pulled it out and looked at the screen.

"Look, Jeeves, I don't want to hear it," I said

before he could chastise me for using magic. The town was turning into an apocalyptic tourist nightmare with reckless impulse-buying zombie consumers that didn't seem to want to take a closed sign for an answer. "I don't know what you all are dealing with at the track, but here in the square, society is starting to break down, dude."

"Fine," he snapped. "Stay safe." The call dropped.

"We need to find somewhere safe to go," I told Spike as I raced toward the back.

* * *

"It's insane down there," I told Liz. "Did you notice when you were coming over?"

"I came through the back alley, not the front, and everything seemed fine back there." She moved toward the window and looked down. "Oh, snap! Look at the square!"

"I don't know that it's safe to stay here. They just broke into old man Rupert's liquor store," I told the assembled group and explained what Spike and I had seen. "If they're starting to break storefront windows—"

"You think they're going to break into an art shop?" Miss Bessie raised her eyebrow.

"This isn't exactly a liquor store, mystic," Mary

quipped.

I glared at them both.

Oh, great.

Now there are two.

"Come on," Spike said, waving at me.

I followed. "Where to?"

"The roof. We're high enough that you can see pretty far," he told me as we made our way to the third floor. "We can take a look around and see if this is concentrated here, or it's everywhere."

We opened the hatch to the roof and heard more glass breaking. Screams of "No, that's mine!" and "You give me that right now!" echoed up from the square. Metal thumps, as if fists were beating on cars, threaded through the cacophony of chaotic sounds.

"Look there," Spike pointed.

The town square was a center of anarchy, but so was the old folks home on the hill. I could see a bunch of elderly residents on the front lawn flinging food at one another while the nurses chased after them. More mayhem at the Holy Grove Church— someone jumped up and down naked on the steeple.

Oddly enough, the prison was a quiet oasis amid multiple points of turbulence.

"There," I pointed, exited. "Look. The library's got no one around."

"Stay here," he said, turning. "Let me make sure."

The ghost floated like a shot toward the Mystic's End Library, a cavernous building watched over by Irma Sperling, the town librarian. Within seconds, he disappeared.

I cringed as I thought of all those old books being torn apart by the crazy mob of rioting happy-demic sufferers. I hoped that little old Irma was safe. "How long before someone impulsively hurts someone else?" I murmured.

It couldn't be long. Things had escalated incredibly quickly, and as if to illustrate my belief, the crunch of metal echoed in the square.

"It's almost empty," Spike said, popping back into view. "There are about twelve people there that are clearly under the influence of whatever this is." He waved his arms. "But the folks at the library are a little calmer."

I frowned. "What are they doing?"

"Reading. They look like they've been there for more than a day. Just sitting on the floor with books piled up all around them. Sitting quietly and reading."

I guess we just answered how many book nerds there were in Mystic's End.

"Okay," I nodded and took a deep breath. "That's where we go."

TEN

"Well, *this* is a surprise," Irma Sperling, the town librarian, said, pushing her horn-rimmed glasses up against her face. She glanced from person to person, her eyes narrow. It was as if she was trying to determine whether we were in a healthy state, or we had come to join the unkempt book addicts in the corner. After a few moments, she nodded. "Since you don't have that glassy-eyed, drooling look about you, I'm guessing you decided this would be a good place to hide out from whatever it is going on out there?"

"It looked quiet." I smiled. It faded quickly when she didn't smile back. "Everything okay here?"

"The casino is packed to the gills with crazy

people pumping quarters into the slot machines. The town square is filled with shoppers waving their credit cards like they're hailing a cab on Fifth Avenue." Irma pointed toward the front of the library. "I have twelve book addicts." Irma looked me in the eye, frowning. "Just *twelve*."

You could have cut the silence with a knife as we stared at the librarian. I couldn't believe the source of her discontent was that only twelve people (locals and tourists alike) found books a worthy compulsion. Liz looked a little dazed, and Pepper looked...well, let's not worry about how Pepper looked. I don't know that she registered anything beyond the pretty colors in the children's section.

Finally, Gabe cleared his throat. "Ma'am, at least you don't have to worry about the library getting damaged. It could be worse."

"The lack of intellectual curiosity in this town laid naked and bare for all to see, and it could be worse, he says?" Irma muttered to herself while shuffling papers on the check-in desk. "It could be worse, he says." She looked up and stared at Gabe. "How could it be worse?"

"This place could be burning down like the Library of Alexandria, Irma—"

"Did I ever say you could call me by my Christian name, son?" Irma snapped.

"Miss Irma, aren't you Jewish?" Liz asked, confused.

"What does *that* have to do with anything?" the old woman retorted with such ferocity Liz jumped. "Back in my day, we showed respect for our elders. Especially when they were clearly having an emotional moment." Irma snapped her head up and shouted, "I'm having an emotional moment!"

Gideon stepped slowly around the check-in counter and walked up to Irma, his eyes bright. Once he padded over to the woman, he pressed his body against her side. She glanced down. He glanced up, his jaw slightly open as if he were smiling. Her shoulders slumped as she dropped down to her stool to cuddle the dog. Within a few seconds, they both let out simultaneous contented sighs.

"I'm sorry," Irma said, her arm still around the supportive greyhound. "Of course you're welcome here. Everyone is always welcome here. It says so right there on the mission statement." She pointed to a plaque on the wall behind her.

Our mission is to make our library a welcoming place to all our community members as we promote a love of reading. We strive to encourage the pursuit of personal interests *through reading and research, to encourage curiosity about the world around us, and to empower people to become ethical users and producers of ideas and information.*

"That's a wonderful mission statement," I told her. "Did you write that?"

"I did," she nodded and pushed her glasses up on her nose again. "I meant every word, too. And look," she pointed to the quiet corner of happy-demic readers. "Twelve whole people agree with me. I thought there'd be at least twenty." She scratched her head and looked to shake off her malaise. Then she glanced over at Pepper. "That's going to be a problem."

"What is?"

"I assumed that Pepper would wind up here sooner or later to try and uncover what craziness has afflicted the town. I already set up a board in the back and pulled books for her." Irma gestured toward the police cage at the back of the library. She glanced back at Pepper—who was sitting on the floor playing with a Thomas the Train set in the children's area—and frowned. "I did not think Pepper would wind up here like *that*."

"Well, at least we know where she's been, and we tested her blood," Gabe told Irma. "So, she is helping in a way. Probably not in the way she would want to, but it's something."

"Well, aren't you suddenly the optimist of the group?" Irma told him sarcastically. She tossed Gabe a massive ring of keys. "Go lock the front door. Let me check on the bibliophiles, and then we'll head to the back."

* * *

Two hours later, we were no closer to uncovering what happened to the town. Still, we did have a list of everything that changed in the two days surrounding the pandemic's start. One was Dalida Dodd's coffee shop opening, two was Martin's father arriving in town, and three was the holiday of Thanksgiving taking place.

Irma felt confident that the holiday itself should be included. Spaniards, she explained, encountered unfortified, dispersed villages composed of individual farmsteads all over Arkansas in the sixteenth century. "Arkansas was home to Native Americans long before Europeans arrived," she explained as her bony finger tapped the whiteboard. "No one here has forgotten what we did to those people, I'm sure—least of all those people still among us."

"You think there's a Native American curse on

the town?" Gabe asked, his voice ringing with disbelief.

"Young man, you're sitting next to a witch, and your ex-girlfriend is crawling around on the floor playing with trains," Irma said, hands on her hips. "Would a curse from a people that honored this land be so hard to believe? They believed in powerful spiritual forces. Maybe those spiritual forces are finally fed up with us."

"Actually, my dad told me that when the Columbus crew brought over greyhounds, they used the dogs for hunting Native Americans," Liz added quietly, her eyes downcast. Gideon hung his head in shame. "I don't know. Maybe we shouldn't dismiss this idea out of hand. Weirder things have happened around here."

Gabe's phone buzzed, and he glanced down at the table. "Ollie's here." He pushed his chair back and grabbed the keys. "I'll go let him in." The phone buzzed again, and Gabe leaned over. He was frowning as he moved toward the front. "By the way, Clutterbuck's still with him."

"Does the chief know you're a witch?" Liz asked me once Gabe was gone.

"No, and I don't want him to know. He doesn't know anything other than what they published in that article in the Mystic's End Herald."

"Well," Liz said, shifting. "This is going to be a little awkward, don't you think?"

The librarian grabbed her paper coffee cup, sipped, and thought for a moment. "Since the police cage is in here, I can't really kick him out."

I sat back. "We just have to be careful about what we say."

"Why do you have to be careful about what you say?" Clutterbuck asked, walking swiftly into the back. Ollie and Gabe followed behind him, looking worried.

"What did you find out from the tests?" I asked Ollie, ignoring the chief of police.

"Nothing." Ollie walked over to his girlfriend, still playing like a toddler on the floor. He kneeled down by her, his face twisted with concern, and smoothed the hair from her eyes. "Hey, babe. How're you feeling?"

"I ate dog food!" she told him proudly. "It had peas in it!"

"Do I want to know?" Ollie looked at me.

I ignored the question. "You didn't find *anything* at all? Not in the coffee, not in her blood?"

"Well, I didn't find anything specifically that was causing it," Ollie said. He kissed Pepper on the forehead, and she blushed and giggled. Standing up, he turned. "I found high levels of serotonin, dopamine, oxytocin, and endorphins. Her cortisone was high, too. Like, high enough that if she wasn't one of the dozens of people experiencing this, I would think she had a tumor or something."

I gasped. "Could she?"

"Possibly, but no cancer cells in her bloodstream."

"So, what do those do?" Liz asked.

"They're hormones. Sometimes called 'happy hormones.' If it was just one of them, you probably wouldn't see this," Ollie said, pointing to Pepper giggling while she flipped through a children's book. "But all of them being abnormally high? They're literally the quartet of chemicals responsible for happiness. Normally, though, they turn off and on. If I had to guess, something's turned them on and jammed them on, so it's continuous. Or," Ollie said, shifting uncomfortably, "they're not turning off, but the brain thinks they have. So the next time the brain switches it on, it's just stacking. I'm not a doctor, though. These are just theories."

"What would do that?" I asked him.

"All four of them plus cortisol?" Ollie shrugged. "Nothing I've ever heard of."

"Is this dangerous?"

"Yes. Absolutely." Ollie nodded, his expression grave. "Those things aren't *just* happy hormones. They control a lot of functions in the body. If these levels get too high, the people afflicted could have a heart attack, a stroke. They may start to hallucinate. I don't know that this is all that's going on here, either. Without taking her to the hospital and running a battery of tests, I just don't know. It's *something* to go on, but I don't think it's the full picture. And without knowing what's causing it?" Ollie glanced at Pepper, his face twisted in frustration. "I don't know how to stop it."

I felt the mood in the room suddenly shift as everyone tried to absorb what Ollie was telling us. The situation had gone from amusing to concerning to a potential catastrophe.

"You're sure, absolutely sure, there's nothing in the water?" I asked Clutterbuck.

"I drank the water after this started," he answered. "I'd be affected."

"Maybe we just have some kind of immunity," Liz suggested. "Can you test our blood for antibodies or something?"

Ollie tilted his head. "Sure. Antibodies to *what*, though?"

"Does anyone know a doctor?" Irma asked.

"If we call a doctor in Little Rock, they'll come in here with the CDC," Clutterbuck said.

"If that happens, Martin's father..." I trailed off. After Jeeves's warning, I didn't know what Don Corleone...er, Salvatore would do. I jumped off my chair and grabbed my phone. "Okay, that's it. I'm calling Jeeves."

"Martin Salvi's bodyguard?" Clutterbuck asked, frowning. "Why would you call him?"

"He's...he's a phlebotomist of a sort," I said as I walked back out toward the front. "You guys get every book you can find on serotonin, dopamine, oxytocin, and endorphins. Medical journals, anything that we can pore over to find a way to tie these together, reverse it, something. I'll be right back."

I heard the group scramble behind me as I walked away.

* * *

"I need you," I whispered into my cell phone, facing the corner of a bookcase. "We're at the library hiding out. Come quick."

"I can't," Jeeves responded calmly. "What's the problem?"

"The problem is the whole town's got elevated hormone levels, probably," I whispered fiercely. "Ollie said this could start killing people. We're stuck, and I need your help."

"What can I do?"

"You told me once you can trace anyone by the

scent of their blood, right? That blood contains an amazing amount of information."

Jeeves paused. "Yes."

"So, that must mean you can tell a lot about the blood itself, right? Who it belongs to, the makeup of it, if they're ill, that sort of thing. Once you drink it, you know a lot—maybe everything—about it?"

Another pause. "Yes."

"I need you to come to do that for Pepper."

Silence. Jeeves was silent so long, I wasn't sure he heard me.

But then, suddenly, he spoke. "Fortuna, am I to understand you are asking me to leave this dire situation here, travel to the library, and *drink* your friend?"

"Not *drink*, this isn't vampire cocktail hour," I snapped. "Just take a little, tiny sip, like you would at a wine tasting." I swallowed once to tamp down nausea I felt at discussing Pepper like this. "Just enough to get the information we need to figure out what's going on with her. With everyone. And how to stop it."

After a few more minutes of silence, Jeeves asked me, "Do you understand what this means?"

"What do you mean?"

"If I do this, I will be bonded to your friend. I will know where she is at all times. I will be able to track her across continents. I will be able to hear her thoughts all the way across town, see through her eyes. She will be unable to block me from her most secret, most private desires," Jeeves paused and waited for me to respond. When I didn't, he continued. "I will ask you once, and only once—do you still wish to make this request of me?"

I knew deep, deep down, this felt wrong. This wasn't a decision I should make for her. But she wasn't in her right mind. Her brain was swimming in hormones and chemicals that made getting her consent impossible. And it wasn't just her. It was hundreds, maybe even thousands of people.

"Do you think you can tell us what's wrong with her?" I asked him.

Another pause. "Likely, yes," the vampire admitted reluctantly.

"It's better than death," I answered, choking back a sob. "How soon can you get here?"

ELEVEN

"You want to do *what?*" Ollie asked, staring at me with a look of horror on his face. He backed up two steps and hovered over his girlfriend, protecting her. "You brought him here so he could *ingest* some of Pepper? Are you *out of your mind*, Fortuna?"

Liz, Gabe, and Irma stared at Jeeves and me with mirrored expressions of horror. Clutterbuck looked confused, as if there was a massive part of the story he was missing. His eyes traveled from face to face to face, as if our eyes would let him know what he didn't understand.

Finally, he demanded, "What, exactly, is going on here?"

Without a word, Jeeves walked over to Terrance

Clutterbuck, passed a hand in front of his face, and caught the large man before he slumped, unconscious, to the Berber carpet below. With a gentle heave, he pulled him to a chair and sat him down as if the large man weighed nothing.

"The two of you really are terrifying sometimes, you know that?" Liz whispered in a frightened voice, her eyes tracking back and forth between the two of us. She hitched her chair away from Clutterbuck and stared at him. "Is he all right?"

"He'll be fine," Jeeves answered. "Eventually."

Liz took a deep breath and nodded. Then she looked away.

"Look," I told Ollie, waving my hands toward Pepper. "You said that we'd have to take her to a hospital for a battery of tests to find out what's causing this, and that might raise suspicion. This is quick, private—"

"Private?" Ollie cut me off. "You think that what you want him to do to her is about *privacy*? Do you know the *first thing* about vampires? You said yourself he's the first one you've met, and he's *not* even a normal vampire!" Ollie shouted, pointing an accusing finger at an amazingly passive Jeeves. "We don't know *what* his powers are because he's part of this organized crime syndicate that uses witches to make sure their power can't be challenged—"

"Ollie?" Pepper tugged on his pants. "Ollie,

why are you so mad?" she asked, looking up from the floor with concern.

"Because your best friend wants to serve you up on a platter to someone I *don't* trust!" Ollie shouted at her. Pepper winced, and tears filled her eyes. "Oh, baby, I'm sorry," he said, rubbing his forehead. He then dropped down to take her in his arms. "I'm not mad at you. I didn't mean to yell at you."

"That's okay. Who am I going to be served up to?" Pepper's eyes lit up through her tears and erased the momentary sadness as if it never happened. "Can you put whipped cream on me? That would be super sexy, right? I *love* whipped cream."

Ollie rubbed his forehead again and stood up, his eyes seeking Gabe. "Don't you have *anything* to say?" Ollie said to Gabe. "You're just standing there, silent. You were with Pepper for years, dude. She's your friend. You've got nothing to say about letting this monster drink her blood?"

"Hey!" I snapped before Gabe could speak. "No need to be insulting—"

"Don't," Ollie warned me. "Just *don't*."

"What the heck's got into you?" I stepped up, but Jeeves lightly placed a hand on my arm.

"*You*, oh great mystic," Ollie retorted. "Did it not cross your mind *once* to come back and talk to us about calling him? Talk to *me*? You know, *before* calling him? She's my girlfriend. Gabe, Liz and I have known her for *years*. You've been here, what, a year tops?" Ollie asked angrily. "I know we're *only* human, and I get that you came from a place where there was a clear hierarchy, always someone in charge. I understand that you lived in a place where the person with the most power just made the rules—"

"Hey, now *wait* a minute!" I told him hotly as I flinched from his uncensored onslaught. "The circus wasn't like that at all! And that's not what this is!"

"Oh, no?" Ollie sneered. "Witches councils, prisons, death sentences for—"

"No!" I shouted. "Charlotte changed all that! She brought a voice and choice back to the paranormal citizens—"

"Did you leave the circus before *you* learned that lesson, then?" he snapped back. "Or is it you just always get more say when deciding between humans and paranormals, Ms. Full Witch? Are we not worth a vote, too? Did you learn nothing from Priestess Goodfellow, or did you just decide you could ignore all that now that *you're* one of the big bads in town?"

We stood across the room and stared at one another. Eyes flickered back and forth on tense faces. You could cut the silence in the library with a precision knife as everyone watched and waited to see what happened next.

I felt attacked. Felt like my history was attacked. Sure, the circuses started as these little dictatorships that flitted all over the world and did what they wanted, but...

Ollie wasn't right that *I* was acting like that.

I frowned.

Was he?

"Ollie..." I started and then stopped. "Ollie, I..."

I wanted to argue with Ollie, wanted to say he was wrong. His ordinarily gentle face was twisted with tension as he stared at me, and I felt more anger coming from him than I'd ever felt before.

And fear.

Fear that if he couldn't change my mind, he wouldn't be able to stop Jeeves...or me.

I wanted to argue with Ollie so much, but suddenly, I realized what he was saying was true.

I took a deep breath. "I'm sorry, I didn't think—"

Ollie exploded. "No kidding! You—"

"Hey, Ollie," Gabe barked. "She got it. You made your point. Throttle it back a bit."

Ollie's head jerked toward Gabe as if he would explode on him, too. He wanted to say something more, something in particular. I could sense it just beneath the surface. See it in the way his skin bunched around his eyes, see it in the pained stare he gave Gabe. Then he nodded once and turned away. "Fine."

I backed away from the group and turned on my heel to get some air.

* * *

I didn't know how long I'd been standing out in the cold evening air when the glass door opened. I didn't turn to see who it was. The complete absence of any emotion, feeling, or thoughts meant it was the vampire.

"Are you all right?" he asked quietly.

"I deserved that." I slid down the brick wall and sat on the sidewalk. "I deserved it, and I earned it. Pepper's not my kid—even though it may feel that way sometimes, considering the way she acts," I chuckled sadly. "But Ollie was right. I should have talked to them about my idea before I called you. I don't even really know why I didn't. Talk to them about it, I mean."

"Don't you?"

I didn't answer.

Jeeves sat down next to me and crossed his legs. We sat silently, overlooking the empty parking lot. In the distance, we could hear fireworks, cheering, and glass breaking. The smell of smoke was in the air. My eyes drifted upward, and I took in the clear, star-filled sky.

"I heard you've been there," Jeeves said, pointing.

"Space? No," I shook my head.

"No, the in-between space that only the circuses can go."

I looked at Jeeves, and he met my gaze. There was an understanding in his eyes, a knowledge I didn't have that was intimidating. "I don't even know that it exists anymore with the circuses gone," I told him, turning a shoulder to him. "But yes, I went a few times. We had to hide there."

More silence.

"I want to say something to you," Jeeves began slowly. "I hope that you don't take it the wrong way, but I feel it needs to be said."

"Okay." I turned to look at him, but his gaze remained fixed on a bag blowing through the parking lot. Jeeves's eyes followed it as it twisted and turned. "What is it?"

"You and I are paranormal, and our solutions to problems will always include all of the available options that we have in our repertoire. For humans, magic will never be anything other than extra-normal. Supernatural. Miracle. It is not a part of their makeup to accept us. Whatever your friend Charlotte did to 'allow' us to assimilate, it will never happen. It cannot happen." He turned and stared into my eyes. "We are not them."

"We're not so different from humans, Jeeves," I told him. "I was a human most of my life. I don't feel that different than I used to."

He cleared his throat and looked uncomfortable. "But we are. Different—quite different—than they are. And at some level, they will always be aware of that. It will always be there between us. Us and humans. Their instinct to fear us as *other* can never go away. It is a part of them the same way our powers are a part of us. When things get tough, get frightening, they will always fear us."

I felt a surge of guilt at his words, shame I had bumbled into Ollie's pain and worry with my arrogance. I might have caused him *more* pain simply because the idea came from me—someone with the ultimate power to force my will if I chose to.

But then I pushed it away.

Jeeves was wrong. They were my friends. It was just a bad night.

Finally, I spoke. "That's an awfully hopeless way to view things."

"Perhaps," Jeeves agreed. After a time, he added, "That doesn't make it any less true."

We didn't speak after that.

* * *

The door swung open, and Gabe stuck his head out. "Can you come back inside?"

"Sure," I nodded, pushing up from the ground. Dusting myself off, I asked about Ollie. "Is he still mad at me?"

There was still a slight tension in Gabe's frame, but it was less than before. "He'll get over it. He's just worried."

"Well, if there's nothing else," Jeeves rose up gracefully, like a gazelle, "I need to get back to Grigio Hills. I don't want to leave Martin alone with his father too long."

"Actually." Gabe cleared his throat and rubbed the back of his neck. "I'm out here to ask you *both* back inside. Can you stay a few more minutes?"

"Why?" I asked, my eyes widening.

"I told you. Ollie's just worried. Ultimately, my mother and grandmother think you should be able to remove the cord between Pepper and Jeeves once we get the information we need. That resolves any concern Ollie has of Jeeves turning her into a zombie or whatever."

Jeeves snapped his head up so fast it could barely be seen as a movement. "Your mother?" he asked Gabe. "What do you mean, your *mother*?"

"The ghosts are back?" I asked, waving at Jeeves to be quiet.

Gabe nodded.

"Wait a minute, please," the vampire said, pink flushing through his face. Jeeves's tone was...almost pleading. It was entirely out of character for him. "How did you contact your mother, Gabriel?"

"Fortuna opened one of the bottles," Gabe said over his shoulder as he walked back inside, holding the door open for me.

With a swift movement, Jeeves pushed Gabe in and closed the door.

"Hey! What the hell, dude?" the detective shouted from inside.

"We'll be a minute. Go join your friends." Jeeves told Gabe through the glass. He moved in front of the door and blocked it, turning with a puzzled look. "The surge of magic the witches felt when I called you, and you hung up on me," he said. "You opened up the witch bottles?"

I nodded. "Just one, though. Not all three. And it was an accident."

"Why didn't you call me?"

"I didn't know you cared about anyone in the bottles other than Martin's mom. It wasn't Martin's mother, so I didn't call you."

Jeeves nodded mutely, his eyes stricken. "So, you *can* open them, then."

"Looks like," I nodded again, confused as to why Jeeves was so profoundly affected. Weren't they, like, totally sure I could open the bottles? I suddenly felt like their confidence in my abilities had been wishful thinking more than anything, because the vampire sure seemed surprised. "We can talk later. You want to step aside so I can get in?"

"What about the other two?"

"The bottles? They're back at my place," I told him. "I'll open them after all this."

Jeeves seemed at a loss for words, and his hands shook almost imperceptibly—a physical manifestation of nervousness I didn't think the stoic vampire was capable of feeling or expressing. The handsome paranormal lifted his face up toward the stars and closed his eyes. I stared at him. If I strained, I could hear echoes of whispers of words— but I couldn't make them out.

"Martin is...pleased," Jeeves told me after several moments, his eyes still closed. "And grateful. Perhaps this will all be worth it, after all."

My eyes narrowed. "What will be worth it?"

Opening his eyes, he half-smiled. "You. You and your demands to make the world a better place."

I didn't know what to say to that, so I said nothing.

As Jeeves opened the door for me, he leaned down close to my ear and said softly, "I will help you solve this issue, whatever it is, with the town."

I leaned my head as far away from the vampire's fangs as I could without making it evident that Jeeves's cuspids were way, *way* too close to my jugular for comfort. "Um. Thanks?"

"In return, you will open the other two bottles at the soonest possible moment. Are we agreed?"

I nodded in reply.

Jeeves followed me as I walked reluctantly, slowly, back to my group of friends. I realized for the first time that the vampire always seemed to walk behind me—as if he could never lay down his need to guard and protect whoever was around him.

Or maybe it was just me.

Maybe this was still Martin's demand he keep me safe.

Or maybe...maybe I still had no idea what the heck was going on in this town.

TWELVE

"Well, it's about time," Miss Bessie scoffed as Jeeves and I made our way back inside. "What took you two so long?"

"Is that the vampire?" Mary asked her mother, pointing to Jeeves who walked in quietly behind me. "My goodness. *He's* quite attractive. I wasn't expecting that."

"That's him." Miss Bessie tilted her head. "Sure, not a bad looking young man, but I don't trust him. We definitely do not want him to have his psychic tendrils in Pepper," she announced, crossing her arms. "Not only isn't it good for her, but it also puts all of us at risk. He'll be able to hear us through her."

"You remember he can hear you now, right?" I raised an eyebrow at the old woman.

"You're suggesting an *absurdity*," Mary told me, her eyes narrowing. "Vampires can't see ghosts."

I bit my tongue for a second before I snapped off a retort I would regret.

It was becoming increasingly evident that Mary Wilcox was *not* the sweetness-and-light angelic figure Miss Bessie and Gabe painted her as. The woman was quick to judge and even quicker to pass that judgment with the same finality her mother had mastered over the years. Mary was acerbic bordering on haughty—only without Miss Bessie's cantankerous old lady charm.

"Ask him," I told her finally, pointing to Jeeves. "Or ask your mother. But I assure you Jeeves can hear and see you the same as I can." I looked around. "Where's Spike?"

Mary leveled a steady stare at me. "We left him back at your shop to make sure no one broke anything."

"He'll come and get us if there's an issue," Miss Bessie added. "Now, we need to talk about your terrible idea. Have you been working on your magic behind my back? Or did you really call that man here to drink your friend with no plan of what to do about the bond after?"

"I didn't know there was anything I *could* do about the bond."

Ollie shoved his chair away from the library table and got to his feet, turning his back to me.

Gabe may be right that he would calm down, but that clearly hadn't happened yet.

"Maybe we should talk over here," Miss Bessie said, her sidelong glance toward Ollie making it clear why she wanted to move. "Tell Gabe and the vampire to stay here—"

"No," Jeeves told the old woman quietly.

"Did you just tell me no, vampire?" Miss Bessie's voice raised an octave or two.

"The three of you are going to discuss manipulating the bond between Pepper and me should I take some of her blood," Jeeves said quietly, his voice passive—but threaded through with a determined will that gave gravitas to his words. "That is not something you're going to discuss outside my hearing. I want to know exactly what Fortuna is planning on doing before I will agree to it."

A sharp pain pierced my stomach, and for the first time, I was nervous. Unless this witch and magic thing concerned art or saving on building construction costs, I didn't use it much. The last time I used magic on a person, I turned Ella Grayson, a murderer, into a greyhound.

Accidentally.

And without knowing how to change her back.

"Fine," Miss Bessie said, her voice stiff. "Not like you wouldn't be able to hear us across the library anyway with your super ears." Turning she smiled. "Now. Have I told you about the silver cords?"

"What silver cords?"

Miss Bessie scrutinized my face and then rolled her eyes. "You and I really have to come up with a formal plan to get you educated on witch magic, Fortuna."

"Really, Mother?" Gabe's mother rolled her eyes. "*I* knew about the silver cords before I was in kindergarten," Mary said sharply.

Mary and Bessie talked about options: how to educate me, how often I would need to practice, where in the woods we should go for larger magics. Once I realized the two women had gone off on a tangent, I cleared my throat.

"While I realize this is incredibly important, I feel like refocusing on solving the issue in front of us is a bit more pressing," I pointed to Pepper. "Not sure if Gabe and Ollie told you, but Pepper's life is in danger. And if her life is in danger, so is everyone's in the town who's afflicted with whatever this is." My eyes darted back and forth between the two women. "Maybe we can refocus on the problem at hand?"

"Oh, it's *just* death," Mary waved her hand dismissively. "As long as no one shoves Pepper in a bottle afterward, she'll be fine. In fact, she might even like it better."

"What are they saying?" Ollie asked Gabe.

Gabe wisely avoided answering the question.

"No, no, Mary, she's right," Miss Bessie said, nodding. "First, I need to know that you can see the magical tie between them."

"But they won't have one until he...you know..."

"They won't, but we *do* have a magical tie right here in this room," Miss Bessie said. She turned and pointed to Gideon, snoring in the corner.

* * *

I rma turned the lights down low and lit candles. Then she placed them in a circle on the floor.

"We don't have *time* for this," Ollie complained.

"Maybe if you had bothered to talk to Fortuna about some of these things, Oliver, we wouldn't have to take the time to do this now," Miss Bessie snapped. She directed me to move a white candle slightly to the right. "I'm certainly not the only magically trained person in this town, am I?"

Gabe's eyes glazed as he listened.

"What's she saying?" Ollie asked again.

"That we have time, and just to be patient. It will be fine," Gabe lied.

Ollie looked at him suspiciously. Turning to me, he asked, "That's not what she said, is it?"

"Quiet, Ollie, I'm concentrating." I snapped my fingers for Gideon and patted the center of the candle circle. "Okay, now what?"

"Now sit across from the dog, and let your eyes unfocus," Mary said in a low, soothing voice, strolling, almost predatorily, outside the circle.

I set aside my growing dislike of Mary and did as she directed. As my eyes unfocused, the air around me seemed to sparkle—like dust particles were catching the candlelight and reflecting it back in tiny golden glows. "I see something," I whispered.

"Let go of your expectation of what's there, of what the greyhound looks like, what you expect him to appear as," Miss Bessie told me. "Look at Gideon with your mind's eye. Don't focus. Don't try to sharpen your view. Just relax and let your image of him go. Open yourself up to what's there."

I breathed deep and tried to relax my muscles, any tension in my body. I tried to force my eyes to unfocus and then realized that wasn't the way to go—I had to drift *away* from control as if I was in one of my painting trances. My shoulders drooped. Gideon glowed as if he was bathed in moonlight.

"Good!" Mary whispered. "Now, between you. Can you see it?"

I could. Between the silvery-white glow we were both bathed in, a cord stretched between us connecting the sparkly magic around each of us. I looked down at my chest. Several cords wove their way out of my body in various places, gathered at my heart, and stretched across to Gideon.

"What is it?" I whispered.

"Before the silver cord snaps, and the golden fountain is shattered..." Mary whispered sadly. The words seemed almost biblical.

"It is the connection," Miss Bessie whispered while she patted her daughter on the shoulder. "You to your own body. You to your magic. You to your familiar. You to the world." The old woman's spirit sighed as if content. "And the inverse to you. Cords can be woven by choice—and cords can be cut by force."

"Isn't that dangerous?" I asked, alarmed. Gideon stepped forward in the circle and licked me. "That anyone can cut these ties?"

"Not *anyone*," Mary said wryly. "Obviously."

"Mary is right, not anyone can cut a cord. Not anyone can forge a bond outside of themselves. But *you* can. And you must if you wish to break the hold that Jeeves will have on Pepper once he does what we all agree he must do." Miss Bessie's serene face hardened, and her voice transformed from gentle to severe. "So, I hope you know how to imagine a pair of scissors, girl."

I shook off the muddled blur and looked up at Jeeves. His face looked troubled. Deeply troubled. "Are you okay with this?"

"Do we care?" Mary asked acidly.

The vampire looked at me for a long minute. Once he spoke, his voice was dark, and his eyes were wary. "Can we speak alone?"

"Oh, for goodness sake, can we just get on with this before I change my mind?" Ollie shouted. "Everyone's so self-protective and calculating—and despite that, the only person in this room right now at serious risk is Pepper! *She* had the idea," Ollie pointed at me. "*You* came running to do it. Now that you'll have your claws pulled out at the end, suddenly, you're not so willing to help?"

"It's not that," Jeeves snapped.

"Really?" Ollie looked unconvinced. "Because I gotta tell you, that's sure what it looks like to me. Are you here to help or *not*?"

"Vampire," Irma said, her eyes sliding back to me for a moment. "If your intention is to find and open all the bottles hidden in this town, you will have to work with the mystic. At some point, you will have to trust." The entire room stared at the librarian, curious looks on their faces. "Can you trust her? Because if you can't, you may as well give up on this quest. You will fail."

Jeeves looked down as I stared at Irma.

"What do you know?" I asked her.

"I know a lot of things," Irma said, spreading her arms wide. "I live in a library the size of a football field. So, *obviously*, I know things."

"Is there *anyone* in this town not keeping secrets?" I asked with exasperation.

"I have a theory about those bottles, that's all," Irma shrugged. "A theory we can't test until we get Miss Pepper back to her old self. So, what do you say, young man?" The librarian held out her hand, palm up. "Is it time to take a drink, or are we going to dance around the necessity and pretend you have a choice in the matter?"

Jeeves stepped toward Pepper, and Ollie jumped in front of him automatically.

"Get out of my way, biker, or we will find out whether the witch is capable of setting a broken arm," the vampire said through clenched teeth. "Move. *Now*."

Ollie's face twisted in frustration. "You hurt her—"

"Yes, yes, I'm sure you'd do your best to try to inflict some level of damage," Jeeves said with some sympathy. He stepped to the side and continued his walk toward Pepper Stanford, investigative reporter and new Thomas the Tank Engine fan.

Before anyone could move, Jeeves closed the five-foot gap between them and leaned down. The vampire passed his hand across her face and whispered, "Sleep."

Pepper collapsed just as Clutterbuck had before.

Jeeves gathered her in his arms and moved his head swiftly down to her neck.

Before I could grasp what was happening, it was over.

"Get her antibiotics, now," Jeeves said, wincing. "Her blood is *filled* with bacteria." He stumbled back and glared at Ollie. "I thought you said you tested her blood?"

"I did!" Ollie responded defensively. "There was no infection in her blood at all! None!"

"It's multiplying at a phenomenal rate, and if it's not stopped, it will take over her body. She's likely only hours away from sepsis. She needs broad-spectrum antibiotics. An injection or IV, if possible."

No one moved.

He turned to Ollie, who was standing frozen. "Now!" Jeeves roared.

Ollie and Gabe raced from the library.

* * *

"This is nothing I've ever seen before," Jeeves murmured. His voice was thoughtful, as if his mind was somewhere far away from the library. "The bacteria are invading every part of her body, it's crossing the barrier of her brain. This is...this is either not natural or—"

"You mean a superbug?" I asked him. "Or like a created bacteria? Wait." I frowned. "Can you even create bacteria?"

"Yes, you can, but no, not like that," he shook his head. "It has an aura to it."

"What do you mean?"

"It tastes like magic," Jeeves said finally.

I frowned again. "What do you mean?"

"Paranormals have a distinct flavor. Their blood is infused with the magic that is a part of them. I can...I can taste it. I can sense it now within her," the vampire said, closing his eyes. "It's churning and roiling within her, playing havoc with her mind, her emotions, her thoughts. She's like a boat tossed on a stormy sea."

As poetic as that was, it didn't help.

Well, it didn't help me.

Irma's eyes lit up as if she just hit the jackpot on a slot machine. "Uh-huh," Irma said, chewing on a pen. "Well, isn't *that* interesting."

Jeeves flashed her a dark look.

"Fortuna, it's time to unhook handsome over there from Pepper," Miss Bessie said. "Probably best to do it while she's asleep."

I looked at Jeeves. "Can you help me carry her to the circle?"

He nodded, and we moved her, gently, to the center of the candles.

As I stood up, I noticed he looked pale and nervous. "Are you sure you're okay with this?" I asked him, not sure what I would do if he said no. I couldn't leave her like this. But still...I felt like I needed to ask him.

The vampire looked up at me with anxious eyes. "You will only cut the cord between Pepper and me?" he asked, a hint of frustration in his voice.

"Of course. I'm not going to go around cutting silver cords willy nilly," I told him as if I cut coil-cords between vampires and humans every day. "I promise I'll be super careful."

He hesitated for a moment and then nodded.

We positioned ourselves across from one another on the floor, the candles still lit. Pepper lay between us. She was gently snoring, and as I glanced down at her, I could not see where Jeeves had drunk from. There were no wounds on her.

I looked up at him.

"I was careful," he said.

I nodded. "Are you ready?"

Jeeves paused and then nodded.

Slowly, with a deep breath, I relaxed my eyes, and the sparkle dust popped up more quickly this time. As I focused my attention on the vampire, he melted into a gigantic, octopus-like miasma of silver cord tentacles reaching out in every direction. Jeeves himself was barely visible beneath them, their sheer volume so overwhelmed the space around him.

"What *is* all this?" I whispered.

"You're only looking for one," he responded in a hard voice. Somehow, I could sense him stiffening. Nervous. The sparkly aura around us both swirled and moved, touching and pulling apart over the peaceful Pepper. "Find it, and let's be done with this."

"My goodness," Miss Bessie whispered, astounded.

Taking another deep breath, I looked down at Pepper. She had a small cord coming from her lower abdomen. I frowned. It wasn't coming from the same place as the one between Gideon and I. Although it clearly lead from Pepper to Jeeves, I was apprehensive about doing anything to it. It wasn't where I expected it.

"You are connected *spiritually* to the dog," Jeeves responded as if he heard my thoughts. "I am

connected *physically* to Pepper. That *is* the cord."
His voice sounded strained, as if this was difficult
for him. "Please," he said harshly, roughly. "Please
cut it and let us be done."

"I'm not sure how," I whispered back. My
fingers opened, and I felt a cold stone placed in my
hand.

"Use that," Irma said. "Think hard about what
you are trying to accomplish, and then cut."

I did.

The cord, which had been taut, split with a
crack. One end snapped back toward Jeeves like a
shot, and the other snaked back into Pepper slowly,
coiling and then, finally, disappearing.

Jeeves lurched out of the circle, heaving as if he
couldn't catch his breath, and scrambled to a
standing position. Pepper yawned and opened her
eyes, smiling wide. Her face looked flushed, and
when I reached down to smooth her hair away from
her face, she was hot to the touch.

"Hi, Fortuna," she smiled. "I love you. You're
such a good friend."

And then she passed out.

THIRTEEN

As soon as Ollie and Gabe returned, I backed away from Pepper and let them work. The two men had an IV bag and needles, and they set up everything with the swiftness of emergency room nurses. I didn't know where they had got it, and I didn't ask. I didn't care.

"Can I help?"

"No," Gabe said, glancing up. "Why don't you go check on Jeeves? We passed him on the way in, and he doesn't look so good. Never seen him like that before." Ollie reached out toward Gabe, and Gabe handed him tools I didn't recognize. "I'm not sure what you did to him, but he looks like he's been through the wringer."

"Are you sure?" I asked him, gesturing toward

Pepper. "She passed out, and—"

"She's going to be fine, Fortuna," Ollie told me
without looking up. "Go check on the vampire.
Gabe's right. He didn't look well." After a short
pause, Ollie added, "We owe him."

The library was quiet. Occasionally, I would
hear a book being dropped to the floor, pages
flipping, the heat turning on and off, but for the
most part, the cavernous warehouse of books felt
silent and empty. It was one more strange aspect of
this town. For each citizen of Mystic's End, there
must have been a hundred books in this place.

I picked my way through row after row of
sturdy bookshelves. I finally found Jeeves sitting in
a reading nook between the back of the library and
the door. He sat with his head in his hands, elbows
on his knees.

"Are you all right?" I asked quietly (in case he
had a headache).

Jeeves leaped up without warning and landed
on his feet in front of me.

"Sorry, I didn't mean to startle you," I said,
stepping back, my eyes wide.

"Nor I you," he answered. "By jumping up
quickly or...or what you saw in there."

I was worried about Pepper. But he sensed
what led my mind when I looked at him. I was
baffled by what I had witnessed in the candle circle.

"Now that you brought that up, what *did* I see in there?"

Jeeves stared at me intently, his eyes unreadable, as we stood facing one another. "I told you once that part of my responsibility is to have as much access to information and insight as possible. The silver cords you saw are my access to that insight."

"All the people you've drunk from."

"Those that are still alive, yes," Jeeves nodded.

I nodded. "When I cut the cord between you and Pepper, why was that so difficult? It seemed like it hurt you, or caused you pain, or something." I tilted my head. "I'm sorry about that, by the way."

"Once I drink, that person becomes part of me. The integration of that person's essence is almost instantaneous," he answered, his head tilting to match mine. "You cut me off from a part of myself. Obviously, that's going to be difficult."

Jeeves was such a strange creature. Most of the time, he gave only the barest of indications he had feelings at all. He could be abrupt and mysterious. Heck, for the first few months I knew him, I wasn't even sure he could talk more than a single word at a time.

And yet what I saw?

He carried and labored under ties to hundreds, if not thousands, of people.

All, I reminded myself, to serve Martin Salvi.

"Thank you for helping Pepper," I said finally, changing the focus of the conversation.

He nodded, and we stood silently, staring at one another.

The silver cords wrapped around Jeeves had been alarming in a way I couldn't describe. Even though I knew nothing about the silver cords before tonight, it bothered me. Somehow, deep inside myself, I knew what I'd seen wrapped around Jeeves like a cocoon was...wrong. Something that shouldn't be. "I hope you're right, and all this is just some weird bacterial infection."

"If it is, you're going to have to do some pretty intense magical work," Jeeves said, frowning. "And I mean no disrespect, but you're not particularly adept at it."

"Thanks, Sparkles," I answered wryly. "What do you mean, though?"

"Bacterial infections *are* contagious. This may be airborne."

"I don't think so," I shook my head. "Gabe and Liz have been around Pepper. Heck, Ollie's kissed her. They haven't gotten infected with the happy-demic. Neither have I."

"You may be immune because you're a paranormal."

"But they wouldn't be," I pointed out.

We stood across from one another, lost in thought again—until Pepper skipped up to the two of us looking healthy and clear-eyed. Jeeves and I gaped at her superhuman recovery in shock.

"Pepper!" I shouted, wrapping her in a tight hug. "You're okay!"

"I'm okay," she squeezed back. "But you two should come back here. We have a lot to talk about."

* * *

Ollie looked elated.

And confused.

"That shouldn't have happened the way it did," he said, pacing in front of the workstations at the back of the library. "Okay, a bacterial infection, sure. Antibiotics should work, absolutely." He stopped pacing and stared at us. "But *five* seconds after hitting her bloodstream?"

"Are you sure it's completely out of her system?" I asked. "I mean, sure, she looks great, and she sounds great, but..." I trailed off as Jeeves tensed.

"Oh, no," Ollie said, shaking his head. "We're not doing that again."

"You hush," Pepper told him, frowning. She walked over to Jeeves, casually threw her leg over his lap, and jumped back onto the table in front of him. "Come on, vampire, want a thigh this time?" Pepper asked seductively, tapping the general area of her femoral artery. "I was so out of it, I barely remember the whole affair. I want my eyes wide open for this one so I can write about it on my blog—"

"You're not writing about this on your blog!" Jeeves, Irma, and I shouted simultaneously.

"Man, I forgot how uptight you guys were," she grumbled, casting an aggravated glance at us. Brightening, she added, "Regardless of the blog post, you *know* I'm right. I need a blood test to make sure whatever was making me act like a loon is out of my system." She pointed down at Jeeves. "He's pretty much the most immediate blood test we have, right?" Pepper tapped her thigh again. "Come on, vampire, right through the denim. It'll be a pair of jeans I treasure forever. Let's go, we don't have all day."

Ollie stared at Jeeves. "If you get *one fang* near my girlfriend's inner thigh—"

"This was not my idea, Mr. Kane." Jeeves's words cracked like snaps of a whip. "I did not place your girlfriend in front of me. I did not suggest the femoral artery. I did not screw up the first blood test so that she suffered for much longer than she needed to. I did not even agree to do this again, so I'd kindly ask you to *put it back in your pocket*."

Ollie's face reddened with fury as Jeeves blamed him for Pepper's lack of diagnosis, and his fists closed so tightly his knuckles turned white.

"Man, this is more fun than being on the happy bugs," Pepper laughed.

"You think this is fun? Are you still infected?" I asked.

"Oh, I am not," she scoffed, waving at me. "I feel a hundred times better than I did ten minutes ago, and I got bit by a vampire and don't even remember it! How many people get bit by vampires and live to tell about it?"

"More than you would think," I told her, shuddering at the memory of all those silver cords. I turned to Jeeves, who looked like he was nailed to the library chair, glaring sullenly at everyone watching him. "Well? Can you think of another way? I know that was hard for you, and I don't want to—"

"It's fine," he said, swiftly shooting up and grabbing Pepper's neck. Again, in the blink of an eye, he was sitting back down in the chair. "She's fine. Though you may want to stop eating so many cheeseburgers. Your cholesterol seems a little high."

Pepper's hands began slapping her neck, her face frowning. "Wait a minute, that's it? I didn't even feel you bite me." Her fingers covered every inch of her neck, frantically looking for teeth marks.

"There's no fang marks. How did you not leave any fang marks?"

Jeeves stared at her, not answering.

"You can bite people without them feeling it, leaving no scars?" Liz asked, again moving her chair slightly away from Jeeves. "And once you do that, you have, like, access to their thoughts and what they see and do and stuff? And they may not even know they'd been bit?"

"Fortuna has that without biting you, and it doesn't seem to bother you in the least bit," Jeeves responded.

Liz stared at him as Chief Clutterbuck let out a loud snore.

"Maybe we should wake him up," I said, pointing to the chief of police, to change the subject. "Pepper's back to normal, and we need to go over the last day before she got sick with a fine-tooth comb. Clutterbuck may have some information that can rule out things he's already looked at, like the reservoir."

"Aren't you *forgetting* something?" Irma asked, pointing at Pepper and Jeeves.

"Oh, right." I looked at the vampire. "Are you ready?"

"Wait, wait, wait!" Pepper said quickly. She grabbed up the candles and blew them out. "I want to keep the tie for a while."

Ollie shrugged Gabe off and exploded at his girlfriend. "You want to *what* now?"

"I didn't really get to experience what it's like to be bit by a vampire—"

"You did, though," I disagreed. "You were bit by a vampire. So, point of fact, you got to experience exactly what it's like to be bit by a vampire. It's just not all that *Twilight* told you it would be."

"Well, it was a little. The vampire's pretty hot and really moody." Pepper smiled and nodded. "Anyway, while you're right, now I want to experience what it's like being tied to a vampire."

"I don't believe this," Ollie muttered, turning away from his girlfriend. "Of all the crazy, harebrained schemes that girl has come up with, this has gotta be—"

"Hey, Ollie," Pepper snapped, suddenly turning serious. "We may have to split up. No one has any psychic ties." She pointed to each one of us. "Other than the ghosts, which only Fortuna can talk to easily, we have distinctly human capabilities here. Yes?"

"Okay, and your point?"

"My *point* is I would've tried to stab you if you took candy from me when I was in that state," she said with sober earnestness. "That I *do* remember. This total lack of a brake on anything I felt, anything I wanted? Everyone else has that. Having him"—she pointed at Jeeves—"be able to tell if I'm in trouble during this might come in handy. Because I have a feeling we're not going to solve this holed up in a library, hiding."

Gabe looked at Ollie. "She has a point."

Irma looked at me, and then the vampire. "Can you and Jeeves not communicate—"

"No," I answered, cutting her off. I reached up and felt for the psychic blocking stone just to make sure it was still there. "No, we can't."

"Interesting," Irma said, her eyes lighting up when she got a new piece of information. "Very interesting." The old woman tapped her glasses and looked deep in thought. "Well, that's for later. In any case, we should take steps to cure the group up front." She frowned. "Though maybe I should wait until they finish the books they're reading. It would be terrible if they were cured in the middle of a good story and then never went back and finished it."

"They could *die*, Irma," Ollie pointed out.

"I'm not sure what's worse," she murmured. She turned away and headed toward the back behind the library counter. "You kids wait here, I'll be right back with something that can help."

* * *

"**B**lowguns?" Gabe asked, incredulous.

"With darts," Ollie said, holding up a dart against the light. "What's in it?"

"Tranquilizers." Irma set a box of darts on the table. "We can empty it and replace it with a small amount of antibiotics fluid. If it works on them like it did Pepper, it should be enough, and they'll be back to normal in no time."

"We can't go around blowing the whole town with blow darts." Liz examined a small blow dart gun.

"Well, no, dear, this is just for non-lethal defense." Irma pushed up her glasses on her nose. "We need to get antibiotics into the reservoir. Pepper still needed to eat and drink when she was under the influence. That should solve some of the problems."

"What about reinfection?" I asked.

"Maybe we'll produce antibodies?" Ollie said with little conviction. "There's really no way to know. This may solve it, though. It's worth a shot." He shrugged. "We can't do nothing."

"We could try and reinfect Pepper again," I suggested.

"Yeah, we could do that," Gabe nodded. "With what, though?"

I frowned. "I can't believe we don't have a clue how this is happening."

"What do you mean, we don't have a clue?" Pepper asked, frowning. "I know exactly where it happened. Well, at least I *think* I do."

"You do?"

"Before I came over here, I went over to the track to play a few slots in the morning," Pepper said. "When I was leaving the casino, I started burping like you wouldn't believe. Big, huge, nasty burps that practically made my throat hurt. My stomach felt like it was filled with gas. Oh, and the burps tasted *nasty*, too," she shuddered. "I'm *positive*, though, that it started in the casino."

All heads swung toward Jeeves.

"I have not been to the track since Don Salvatore showed up," Jeeves told us quietly. "If this originated there, I could not tell you how or why."

"You're sure?" I asked Pepper.

"Sure as a heart attack. Which I almost had, apparently," Pepper said.

"Then we go there and see what we can find."

"Armed with blow darts!" Irma held out the blowguns.

"What about him?" Gabe hitched his head toward his old boss.

"I will awaken him." Jeeves stood up. "He needs to ensure that antibiotics get into the reservoir. Those of you that wish to can accompany me to the casino. We'll see if we can get to the bottom of this."

FOURTEEN

"That's quite a story," Clutterbuck said for the third time from the back of the van. I was getting the feeling he didn't believe us or...no, it was just that. He didn't believe us. "And y'all are telling me that I just slept through this whole discussion on the problem, y'all finding a solution, and Pepper going from crazy to totally sane?"

"Well, I wouldn't say I'm *totally* sane, but I'm back to normal for me," she answered cheerily. I glanced in the rearview mirror and saw Clutterbuck's expression. It was somewhere between disbelief and outright suspicion.

"And I *slept* through all this? Just took a nap in the middle of a crisis? On a hard library chair?"

I kept my hands on the wheel and brought my attention back to the road. Though the streets around the library were relatively quiet, occasionally, a reveler drunkenly shot out in front of the van, headed from one place to another. I needed to pay close attention so I didn't squash someone with the truck.

"Watch that guy," Gabe murmured from the passenger seat.

"I see him."

"Look, the important thing is we found a cure," Pepper said. "That's what you were after, anyway, right? Some way to cure your daughter?"

"I *am* the Chief of Police, Ms. Stanford," Clutterbuck informed her—as if we all weren't aware of his position. "Just because my primary concern is Rowena—er, Evangeline—doesn't mean I'm not concerned with everyone else in this town as well. How're we going to cure all these people and the tourists with some blow darts?" He held up one of Irma's blowguns. "We'll be shooting people with these things for weeks."

"The reservoir," Gabe called toward the back.

"It took almost nothing for Pepper to come back after we gave her the antibiotics," Ollie explained. "No time, not much of a dose. It seems like this bacteria, whatever it is, is particularly susceptible to the smallest amount of antibiotics. If we put the antibiotics in the water, we should be able to get most of the town over the next few days."

I could feel Clutterbuck's incredulity hitting me in waves.

"I don't mean to be obtuse, here, but how is that even possible?"

"We don't know," Pepper said, shrugging. "But for the moment, the how doesn't matter. The fact that it works? That's what matters. We can worry about why later. After we save people."

That seemed to lay it on the line for him, and the gruff police chief nodded. He shifted, and I glanced back to see him pulling out his phone from his pocket. "Can we take a detour to the hospital? That seems to be where Evangeline is. I'd like to get her treated as soon as possible. We can also inform the hospital what they need to do if patients show up."

"On it," I called back, turning.

"How do you know where your daughter is?" Pepper asked curiously. "Did she text you?"

"Uh, no," he answered quickly. Too quickly. I felt a flush of embarrassment coming from the chief, and I knew, instantly, what the chief of police was so embarrassed about.

"Oh, you do *not* have an app on your adult daughter's phone, so you can track her, do you?" I called back loudly. "That is just gross! She's an adult, Clutterbuck, not a child."

"Have you seen how much my daughter can drink?" Clutterbuck barked back. "If she gets into trouble, I have to be able to find her. You mind your own business, Delphi! This doesn't concern you!"

The van fell silent as we continued our slow, methodical crawl toward the hospital.

"Hey," Pepper asked, her voice low. "What app do you use? Is it a police thing, or can anyone get it?"

The two talked in low tones as Gabe, and I smiled at one another. It was good to have Pepper back to her old self. Even though I was worried about how we would solve the problem with the town, having something seem ordinary again was a reason to celebrate.

* * *

The hospital was quiet.

"Where the heck is everyone?" Ollie asked no one in particular as he walked into the waiting room. No one was in the reception area, and the waiting room was empty.

"Evangeline?" Clutterbuck bellowed. "Evangeline, honey, are you here?"

"Daddy!" A screech echoed from the hallway

toward the emergency room area. Heels clicked against the floor as a haggard, makeup-smeared woman raced toward us. "Daddy, I'm going to be a doctor! I helped three people when they came into the emergency room!"

"Did you, now, pumpkin?" Clutterbuck asked his voice tense. The chief of police was slowly loading up his blowgun with a dart and looking at his daughter with a pained expression. "I'm very proud of you, sweetheart."

I didn't know *why* he was proud of her. Letting a drunk Evangeline Laroux loose in an emergency room with access to a scalpel seemed like a recipe for disaster. I fully expected to find three bleeding bodies in the place.

"Angie, stand still," Pepper called.

Evangeline turned toward her voice, and Pepper hit her square in her right breast with a blow dart.

"Ow!" Evangeline screeched and pawed at her chest. Suddenly, she froze. "Oh, my." Her face turned white and she reached frantically for a chair. "I'm a little woozy," she said, sitting down. Frowning. "My insides suddenly feel hot."

Clutterbuck raced over to his daughter, shooting Pepper a nasty look on his way.

"You just couldn't help yourself, could you?"

Gabe commented, but his expression was vaguely amused.

"Honestly, Clutterbuck looked like he was about to have an emotional breakdown," Pepper shrugged. "I thought I could get it done faster and save him the emotional trauma of blowing a hole in his only daughter. Even if it was just a tiny hole."

"That was really nice of you."

"I *can* be nice, Gabe." Pepper looked at him full-face as Ollie moved in the direction Evangeline had come from. "Just because I'm not nice to you much doesn't mean that I'm not nice in general. You're a special case," she told her ex-boyfriend.

"Honey, are you *sober?*" Clutterbuck asked his daughter. Pepper, Gabe, and I turned to stare at the father-daughter pair. "Your eyes are clear, your face isn't blotchy. You look positively healthy."

"You say that like you've never seen me sober before," she retorted acidly.

Clutterbuck cleared his throat but didn't respond.

"What's *she* doing here?" Evangeline asked, jabbing her finger in my direction.

Apparently, her sobriety did nothing to dim her hatred of me.

"I needed her help."

Turning, she frowned. "Why didn't you just go ask Martin for help?"

Martin? Why would the chief of police go to Martin for help when we just realized that Pepper got ill at the track not even an hour ago? I examined Angie's face, but her expression revealed nothing— well, nothing other than contempt for me.

Which, you know, was a given at this point.

"I ran into Fortuna at the new coffee shop, pumpkin. They were already investigating, so we teamed up," her father told her. He was about to say something else, and then he hesitated. I could read in Clutterbuck's mind—he was going to mention my psychic ability, but then decided not to. He believed it would set Evangeline Laroux off, and he didn't want to deal with it. "Gabe handled one of the first cases in the town."

"Yeah, okay, so you should have worked with *Gabe*," Clutterbuck's daughter snapped at him. "Not *her*."

"I'm going to see what Ollie's found," I told Pepper and Gabe, and then I walked away before I could hear any more. I looked back once more to find a sullen Evangeline Laroux shooting imaginary daggers across the lobby at me.

* * *

"Someone tied him up," Ollie said as he slowly undid masking tape from a white-coated doctor's wrists. His badge announced his name to be Reese Arnhem, the head of emergency medicine at Mystic's End Hospital. "It took me a bit to find him." Ollie hitched his head toward a metal locker. "Someone shoved him in there."

"Is he infected?" I answered.

"I don't think so. At least his eyes seem pretty clear, skin doesn't feel hot. I want to get his wrists first, and then I can get the tape over his mouth." The doc's eyes widened in terror. "Um, or he can do it."

Dr. Arnhem nodded vigorously, and I could feel gratitude pouring off the man. It took three or four minutes of careful peeling to get the sticky tape off his skin without ripping out too much hair. Once his hands were free, the doctor peeled the tape from his mouth, wincing all the while.

I eyed him up and down. "Are you okay?"

"Some water, please?" Dr. Arnhem asked us in response.

Ollie walked into the hallway and quickly returned with a cold bottle of water. The doctor drank it as if he'd been lost in a desert for days.

"Thank you," he said after downing the entire thing. "I've been tied up like that for a few hours, and I was becoming dehydrated." He looked back and forth between us, confused. "Are the two of you patients here?"

"No, we're here with the chief of police," I told him, nodding toward the hallway. "We had a friend that was affected by whatever this thing is that's going around, and we discovered that antibiotics knock it out in, like, five seconds flat."

"Well, young lady, that's impossible," the dark-haired doctor told me, frowning. "Antibiotics need time to work." He looked at Ollie more closely. "Aren't you the coroner?"

"Assistant coroner, yes," Ollie nodded. "And I hear what you're saying, but my girlfriend was acting all crazy like everyone else. The moment I stuck her with an IV, she got better. And I mean *the moment*. Almost as if she'd never been sick. I've never seen a recovery that fast before, but I saw this one with my own eyes."

"We just gave Evangeline Laroux a minuscule amount of broad-spectrum antibiotics through a blow dart," I told him as the three of us walked back toward the lobby. "The same thing happened. And back at the library, too. There were a bunch of folks there, and antibiotics cured them almost instantaneously."

The doctor still looked skeptical. "But that shouldn't work."

"Whether it should or it shouldn't, it did, and I don't think we have time to debate it," Ollie told the doc, and he explained what we'd found.

Just not how we found it.

"Reese!" Clutterbuck called as we reentered the lobby. "Am I glad to see you."

"Terry, are you with these folks?" the doctor asked.

"For the moment." Clutterbuck gave a sharp nod. "They told you what we think is going on?"

Dr. Arnhem nodded and strode over to Evangeline Laroux. Pulling his penlight from his pocket, he shined it in Angie's eyes, had her open her mouth so he could peer in, and took her pulse. "Her pulse is much lower than it was when she came in here," he said, glaring at her. "Though I suppose tying up and taking an entire medical staff hostage can cause some excitement."

The chief turned and stared at his daughter. "That was you?" Clutterbuck asked incredulously.

"It's not like the hospital's very big," she said, shrugging. "It was *only* three people."

"There are two more people tied up?" I asked alarmed.

"Come on." Ollie grabbed Angie's hand. "Show me. Let's go get them out."

Evangeline Laroux stomped off like a small child that had just had her toy taken away. Clutterbuck and Arnhem continued talking, and the chief confirmed for the doctor what Ollie had just explained.

While I listened, I realized that I hadn't seen the vampire a single time since we entered the hospital. Scanning down the corridors of the waiting area, I frowned. "Hey, where's Jeeves?" I asked Gabe.

Gabe swung his head around and looked. "No idea. Haven't seen him since we got here."

"I have three or four people here that I can treat," Dr. Arnhem was telling Chief Clutterbuck. "If they haven't gotten out of the restraints, anyway. What do you need?"

"Antibiotics." Clutterbuck hitched his head toward the door. "We're going to take them and dump them in the reservoir just before the outlet. If people hardly need any, hopefully, that will take care of the majority of the infections."

"Sounds like as good a plan as any." Dr. Arnhem lowered his voice and looked up at the police boss with a look of grave concern. "Terry, how did this happen? Was this on purpose? Some sort of attack?"

"I don't know, Reese. I just don't know. We're still looking into that."

When Clutterbuck looked at me, I could tell the chief wanted to tell the doctor more, but he was frustrated that he didn't know more. And he blamed me for that.

"Hey, something you probably should know,"

Dr. Arnhem said, stepping closer to his friend. "The mayor was in here earlier today."

Clutterbuck's eyes shifted back to his friend. "Mirabelle Saunders came here? Why, was she sick?"

"No, she wanted to talk to me about what was going on in the town." The doctor glanced around nervously—as if he was concerned he would be overheard. "She told me not to worry about people getting a little out of control this holiday season." His gray-stubbled chin was raised as he looked Clutterbuck in the eye. "Ter, I swear, it sounded like she knew what was going on. Told me not to worry, that everything would be fine and that this holiday season would do great things for the town."

"Maybe if you work for the sanitation department and you need the overtime. Otherwise, not so much," Clutterbuck said gruffly. His jaw clenched. "How could that woman possibly know this would happen?"

"I don't know." Reese's eyes darted down one hall, then another, and then another. "I wish I knew. Let me get those antibiotics for you."

"Thanks."

"Damn it. I really should stay here, but if what you said is true,"—Dr. Arnhem glanced around for Ollie, but he hadn't returned yet—"I really need to get over to the old folks home and check on them. If this is an infection, it's going to hit them harder and faster than anyone else." He looked around. "Thing is, I'm the only doctor here tonight, and I couldn't get through to either of the two ER docs before."

"We can do that," I told him.

"We can't," Pepper pointed out as she walked back into the room. "We need to get to the reservoir."

"Maybe we should split up."

"The chief and I can go to the reservoir," Gabe volunteered. "You and Ollie and Jeeves can go to the home and check those folks." Gabe frowned. "It seemed to me that the whole place had gone nuts, so it may take all four of you to administer the doses."

"Jeeves will be back in a minute," Pepper announced.

I raised my eyebrow. How did she know he would be back in a minute?

"He had to stop at the bank," she told me, her eyes skipping over to a sign on the wall.

I'll let you guess what kind of bank the sign pointed the way to.

FIFTEEN

"Am I just being paranoid, or does it seem like Evangeline Laroux is on the periphery of almost every weird situation in this town?" I asked Pepper as we drove slowly toward Mystic Memories Senior Living Center. The reporter sat in the passenger seat this time, Ollie leaning between us. "She was at the hospital tying up doctors and nurses—that doesn't seem weird to you?"

When I moved to Mystic's End, Evangeline Laroux seemed like a strange, pseudo-glamorous creature. Not someone I would want to be friends with or anything, but something fascinating to look at. Like human art.

With platinum hair and a Jayne Mansfield

smolder, the owner of *the Club* held court at her restaurant each night as if she really was the movie star she had tried (and failed) to be in Hollywood. The more I got to know the former Rowena Clutterbuck, the less I was dazzled, and the more I was disgusted. The man-chasing boozy daughter of the chief of police came back to Mystic's End after her elderly husband of hardly any time died, leaving her millions.

Despite her money, her business, and the attention from every male within a five-mile radius, Angie never seemed happy.

And when face to face with me, she could turn downright venomous.

"Nothing Rowena Clutterbuck does is weird to me anymore," Pepper told me, pointing to a woman dressed in a bathrobe and curlers crossing the street. "That's a woman operating on her own set of rules and timetables." Rolling down the window, Pepper casually blew a blow dart at bathrobe woman. "Got her."

"Nicely done, honey. I don't think she knows who she is, honestly," Ollie added about Evangeline while pointing at a swaying man carrying a cake as he stepped out into the road. "When her mom died, she took it really hard. I don't think she ever got over it."

I frowned as Pepper took aim with the blowgun.

Did I know her mom was dead, too? I was losing track of the string of mothers killed in this town. "Pepper, is your Mom alive?" I asked out of the blue. "You never talk about your parents."

"Yeah, she lives in Albuquerque. She and Dad moved to New Mexico. She read some articles about the benefits of living at high altitude, and within a few weeks, they were gone."

"That was kind of impulsive."

"Now you know. I come by it honestly," Pepper said gracefully, rolling down the window and blow-darting another citizen. "But no, if you're wondering if I'm part of the Dead Mothers Society in this town?" I winced at the unofficial nickname and glanced at Ollie in the rearview mirror. He didn't seem particularly bothered by it. "I am not. My mother's very much alive. Why?"

"I was just curious. Like I said, you never talk about your parents."

"There's not much to talk about. I had a happy childhood. My parents were quiet academics that loved and cherished me. They expected a lot, they disciplined without being all rage-y. It's not a terribly interesting story—if you know what I mean. Not like Ollie over here." Pepper hitched her thumb back toward her boyfriend. "Maybe if I had a father that was a cult leader, I'd tell more stories."

"My father's not a cult leader," Ollie told her,

his hand tapping her affectionately on the head. "Yes, the church is a little weird. You notice I don't get up early on Sunday mornings. But Holy Grove Church isn't a cult. It's just got some weird beliefs. And, I mean, you can say that about any religious organization, really."

I had been to Holy Grove Church once. Cult seemed a valid descriptor.

"Oh my gosh, what is going on up there?" Pepper whispered. She craned forward and looked up the driveway to Mystic Memories Senior Living Center. "Is that Harold Whatnow running around naked?"

It was indeed my grumpy art student, Harold Whatnow, at the top of the hill. The skinny old man looked down at us, arms high in the air and hips thrust forward. He was hooting and jumping slowly up and down.

"Well, *that's* not something I'll ever be able to unsee," I told Pepper and Ollie.

Ollie tried to stifle a laugh. "Hon, do you want to hit him with a dart, maybe?"

"Can we get a little closer?" Pepper told Ollie nervously and then swallowed. "My aim is getting better, but...I mean.... Can we just get a little closer, please?"

I drove up the road.

* * *

The Mystic Memories Senior Living Center lawn held small clusters of elderly folk. They were sitting in circles on the ground like teenagers in a park, passing bottles of alcohol back and forth. They looked happy—that glassy-eyed happy we had come to recognize as a side effect of the bacteria—but were relatively sedate compared to what we'd seen from a distance earlier.

The three of us picked our way through, blowing darts at each person we came across. Because these folks were older, some with medical conditions, we paused after each "attack" to check on our targets. Thankfully, the antibiotic darts seemed to have the same effect on them as they did on the others we had rehabilitated. After a few woozy moments, the residents of Wrinkle City seemed fine.

Confused about what happened to them, but fine.

"I was wondering when you would get here." Uncle Vito walked out the front door and made a beeline toward us. His eyes were clear, and his face grave as he strode purposefully across the front yard. He didn't seem affected by whatever this was, but I didn't know what a former mobster would turn to in a moment of complete freedom. So I was a little wary.

Stepping back, I stared into his eyes. "You're not affected?"

"Nope. My nephew had one of the drivers take me back, and when I saw how people were acting? I locked myself in my room and didn't come out," the old gangster told us, tipping his hat. "I got some snacks and bottled water in there, so I was fine. I saw you come up the way, so I came out."

"You have surveillance cameras in your nursing home room?" Pepper asked, her eyes wide.

"*Assisted living facility*, girly. I don't need a nurse," Uncle Vito corrected her. "If I did need a nurse, I wouldn't have one, though. They went over the edge with the rams just like the rest of 'em."

I blinked. "They went over the *what* now?"

"I'm coming!" Harold Whatnow shouted loudly. "Just hold your horses, I'm coming!"

"No one called you, Whatnow!" Uncle Vito called back to his friend. "Why don't you go inside and lay down? You had one helluva night."

"I don't need to lay down," Harold barked back.

"Then why don't you go inside and cover up that shriveled noodle of yours?" Uncle Vito pointed to Harold's family jewels. The naked old man stared at him in confusion. "You're lucky it ain't spring. That's a bad place to have a mosquito bite."

"What are you talking—" Harold cut himself off as he looked down and realized he was buck naked. He brought his hands forward quickly to cover himself, and his entire body flushed pink. "Where are my clothes? Who took my clothes?"

"Go get dressed," Uncle Vito told him again, pointing to the doors of the home. "You two," Vito said to Ollie and Pepper. "There're going to be a few more still in crazy town that need healin'. Can you take Harold back to his room? He's annoying as hell, but he's still my friend. I don't want him to get hurt. Besides, I need to talk to Fortuna." Uncle Vito paused. "Alone."

Ollie looked back and forth between us and nodded. "Come on, hon."

Pepper's expression denoted that she did not want to leave, and she really wanted to know what Uncle Vito would say. She stood immobile, biting her lip and glancing back and forth between Ollie and Uncle Vito. Finally, she stomped her foot and took Ollie's outstretched hand. The two went over to Harold and escorted him inside.

"That girl doesn't like to miss anything," the old man said, amused.

"No, she doesn't," I agreed. "What did you want to talk to me about?"

"You know that visit to your art studio was just

about Martin's father getting a gander at you, right?"

"I didn't precisely know that, but I figured it was something like that."

"I'm gonna tell you something I'm not supposed to," Uncle Vito said. The old man stepped closer, and I could smell his Drakkar Noir cologne. "Now, I'm not passing judgment on you for making Martin swear he would end greyhound racing. I understand why you did it. Hell, I even kind of agree with you. That's no life for a dog."

I tilted my head. "I'm sensing a 'but' here somewhere."

"Well, here's what you don't know," he said, folding his arms over his chest. "My nephew doesn't know that his son came to this town looking for the bottles. Hell, Marty doesn't even know that Martin *knows* about the bottles. He made Addie swear never to tell Martin, and he assumed she would keep her word since the consequences of not keeping your..." Uncle Vito let the implication hang.

"But she did tell Martin, and she didn't keep her word," I guessed.

"Well, not at first. Martin wondered why his aunt kept coming to this town, taking long vacations. She never seemed to have any stories of digging up crystals or going out on the lake. You

know, the reason people used to come here before
the track. Old Addie's a sweet woman, and she
doesn't do cagey very well, bless her heart." Uncle
Vito smiled affectionately. "Eventually, Martin
followed her. When he had enough information, he
confronted her. That's when she told them."

"Them?" I asked.

"Martin and Jeeves."

Of course.

"So, you see, Martin's been pulling a fast one on
his father. And my nephew is not one that takes
kindly to people not telling him everything."

I frowned. "Pulling a fast one how?"

Uncle Vito stared up at me, his arms still folded.
"Marty Salvatore knew about the bottles."

"Okay," I answered, still not understanding.

"Marty Salvatore never told his son Martin
about the bottles," he added.

I could see how upset that could make Martin.
But I could see a hundred reasons Marty Salvatore
might have withheld this information from his son.
Just because he was a mafia guy didn't mean his
reasons had to be nefarious. Right?

"Maybe he just didn't want Martin to be upset.
I mean, I don't know that *I'd* be really thrilled to
find out that my mother's soul was locked in a bottle
for all eternity."

"Or maybe he didn't want his son to know that he

had the power to open the bottles and wasn't going to," Uncle Vito said with finality. My eyes widened in shock. "Maybe the Mafia King didn't want his son to rebel against him, didn't want the heir to the family to figure out the secrets that killed his mother."

"Wait a minute. Wait a minute. What do you mean 'open the bottles'? I thought the mystic was the only one that could open the bottles."

"Any door can be opened in a multitude of ways, yeah? You may be the key, girly, but a battering ram can take a door down, too, if you don't have the key. Know what I mean?" Uncle Vito stared up in my face, one eyebrow high on his forehead. "That man has over a hundred witches on his payroll. You don't think he could've gotten his wife out of the bottle if he wanted to?"

Uncle Vito was telling me that—for some reason—Marty Salvatore Sr. was just fine with his beloved wife being cursed. He was just fine with the mother of his child being imprisoned in a bottle. Forever. And what's more, he extracted oaths to make sure his son would never find out.

"When did he find out that Martin knew about the bottles?"

"He *doesn't* know," Uncle Vito said. "Well, not for *sure*. He suspects. And I gotta tell you, Fortuna, I'm not sure which is more dangerous. Him being suspicious Martin has turned on him, or him knowing for sure that Martin has." Uncle Vito looked down and then back up into my eyes. "What I *can* tell you is he's here for two reasons."

"And those are?"

"To remind Martin who's in control here. And to find out what's going on in this town that Martin's not telling him."

* * *

After blow-darting everyone at the Mystic Memories Senior Living Center, the three of us climbed back into the van. Gideon was still sleeping in the back, snoring, as if nothing strange was going on that the dog needed to be concerned about. We left the nurses with instructions to give anyone showing symptoms antibiotics stat. Uncle Vito promised to call if the home went off the rails again.

I pulled the van over once we were out of sight and filled Ollie and Pepper in on what Uncle Vito had told me.

"So, wait, he's here because you wanted to end greyhound racing? Or because you're looking for the witch bottles?" Pepper asked, confused.

I thought back to the conversation and frowned.

"I don't know. Uncle Vito kind of meandered there a little bit."

"I don't know that it matters. Based on what you just told us, Marty Salvatore could be here because he doesn't want greyhound racing stopped, or he could be here checking on the bottles. Either way, he's not here for anything good," Ollie pointed out. Then he frowned. "I don't understand why your agreement with Martin to end greyhound racing would matter to him, anyway. I thought Martin owned the track?"

"There are so many shell companies involved in the ownership of the track it would make your head spin," Pepper said, turning toward him. "It's impossible to know who really owns the track. It was one of the first things I looked into when I started getting into journalism. I mean, until Fortuna got here? I didn't even know that Martin was Don Salvatore's son. Or that Jeeves was a vampire."

Ollie frowned and gave her a look. "I'm still not happy you did that. I think you need to let Fortuna untether you from him."

"Oh, calm down." Pepper rolled her eyes. "It's actually kind of cool. I can concentrate really hard and know where he is. I can even talk to him a little bit—though the farther away he gets, the harder it becomes."

Ollie's eyes narrowed. "Where is he, anyway? Wasn't he supposed to come with us?"

"He went back to check on Martin."

"Is Martin okay?" I asked her.

"I can't tell you that. Like, I can tell you what Jeeves thinks, but I can't tell you if Martin's *actually* okay. Just whether Jeeves *thinks* he's okay." Pepper looked at Ollie again, and this time it was Ollie rolling his eyes. "You really have to get over yourself. I don't know that I'm giving this up. It's, like, the first superpower type thing I ever had. I kinda want to keep it."

Ollie glared at her.

"Can you guys do this some other time?" I asked with some exasperation. "I just want to know if Martin's okay."

"I told you," Pepper repeated, holding up her hands. "I can't tell you if Martin's okay. Only if Jeeves thinks he's okay."

"Well, *does* Jeeves think he's okay?"

"Nope."

SIXTEEN

We were back on the road.

Sort of.

It was a slow, careful crawl through the streets of Mystic's End. As we moved down rural roads on the outskirts of town surrounded by trees, everything *almost* seemed peaceful. Just when I thought we were hitting a calm stretch, glassy-eyed citizens would pop out and race in front of me like they had a death wish.

I would slam on the brakes, and Pepper would slither out the passenger side window. Ollie held on to her legs to keep her from tumbling out while she took aim and fired. We must have performed the same feat a dozen times or more.

"I almost don't want to admit it, but this is kind

of fun," Pepper announced. She sank back down into the passenger seat and rolled up the window. "I mean, I wouldn't want to go attack people with blow darts on a random Saturday or anything. But I'm getting good at this."

"You're a blowgun natural, Pepper," I agreed as we slowly crept forward again.

"How are Miss Bessie and Mary getting along?"

"I don't know," I told her as I scanned for party people. "I haven't seen them since the library. Wait, were they at the library?" I thought back. "Oh, yeah, they showed up at the end. And then they disappeared after Jeeves and I went in the circle," I said, frowning. "Anyway, I haven't seen them since then."

"That circle thing was wild," Pepper murmured, scanning intently. "What is she like, anyway? Gabe's mom? Whenever he talked about her after she died, he always made it sound like she was some kind of angelic, forgiving, loving person. And it's weird, but I don't remember that too much from when we were kids. I remember being kinda scared of her."

"To me, she seems like a younger version of Miss Bessie. She's beautiful but harsh. She even seems a little harsher than Miss Bessie," I admitted. I thought about the unsparing stare the ghost cast in my direction repeatedly. "She definitely doesn't seem to like me much."

"From what *I* could gather, she thinks you left her in a bottle," Pepper pointed out. "You have to admit her perspective may be a little jaded due to that. Besides, she just doesn't know how much Gabe likes you yet."

"Well, I don't need parental approval to be friends with someone."

"Friends. Sure." Pepper snickered. "That's what you and Gabe are."

I slammed on the brakes as I spotted another drunken group making its way across the roadway. Pepper let out a yelp and turned with narrowed eyes.

"Jeez, I'm sorry! It's not like everybody around you and Gabe doesn't see that the two of you are gonna wind up together eventually. Still, I'll keep my mouth shut if you'd prefer to pretend that's *not* true!"

"I didn't stop the car because of that!" I pointed toward the front windshield. "Shiny happy zombie people at twelve o'clock? Did you want to just leave them that way? Run them over?" I was a little snarkier then I needed to be, but I had just got Miss Bessie to stop haranguing me about being destined for Gabe. I couldn't believe that Pepper might be picking up the old woman's mantle.

"Oh, right, sorry." Pepper shimmied out the window as Ollie grabbed her calves.

* * *

It'd taken us an hour to go three miles. As we turned a corner, Pepper whispered, "Stop! Pull over! Over there, in the bushes! And quick, shut off the lights!"

I did.

"You want to tell me why we're hiding here?" I asked, straining to see what she saw.

"That's Mayor Saunders's house," Pepper whispered, pointing.

At the other end of the small pasture to our right, a large ranch house was lit up brightly. The fence wrapping around the large property was extra high but see-through. "Is that an exotic animal fence?" I asked, recalling a drive-through safari I'd gone to that had similar fencing.

"Saunders buys exotic animals."

"Why?"

"Because she can? I don't know." Pepper squinted. "She's got wild goats, Himalayan tahrs, wildebeests. I think there's even a giraffe back there, some zebras. Anyway, is it my imagination, or is that a limousine parked over there?"

The three of us leaned forward and squinted.

"The mayor doesn't have a limousine," Ollie said. "At least, I'm pretty sure she doesn't."

"So, let me ask you a question," Pepper said, turning. "Would Don Salvatore fly here like a normal person? Or would he, like, teleport here somehow? Do you know?"

"They had a huge communication cauldron in the witch room at Martin's," I told her, thinking back. "Do you remember when you first realized I was a witch? You saw an arm sticking out of the tiny little cauldron in my bedroom?"

Pepper shuddered. "Unfortunately, I remember."

"They have one that comes up to my waist. It's huge. They could bring twenty people through there in a line. Fifty people. Easy." I stared at the front of the black limousine, trying to determine whether it was one of the track's fleet. Those usually had a blue medallion on the front, but I was too far away to see. "There'd be no reason for him to fly here or drive here unless he needed to for some other reason. That would be my guess."

"Does Martin give the mayor use of the limos?" Ollie asked.

"I don't know. Wouldn't that be, like, improper influence or something?" I asked.

Pepper laughed. "This whole town runs on improper influence, Fortuna."

"Hey, pull the van up about ten feet," Ollie said, pointing. "I thought I saw something on the porch, but at this angle, I can't get a good look. It's like something was moving. Like someone's standing there."

"If I start the van, we might attract attention," I told him.

"There's a house right over there behind us." Ollie pointed. "I think we'll be okay."

I nodded and turned the van on. Putting it into drive, we crept forward slowly.

Ollie gasped.

I slammed on the brakes.

"What is it?" Pepper asked him, turning back and forth between Ollie and the house. "What do you see? I can't see anything, it's so dark."

"There are two men on the front porch."

"The mayor's husband, Brent?" Pepper asked.

"No, I don't know them," he responded. "But they're armed. Both of them. Those are armed guards. I'd bet my life on it."

"Well, let's *not* do that," Pepper said, patting his arm.

Suddenly, light filled the interior of the van. It was coming from the direction of the porch, and I instantly sensed suspicion coming from the two men Ollie had spotted.

Pepper let out a string of curse words that made even Ollie wince.

"We're blown, we gotta go," I said, throwing the van into drive and pulling back onto the road. Instead of going fifteen miles per hour, I did a speedy twenty-five.

"Can you go any faster?" Pepper jumped out of the seat, pushed Ollie aside, and raced to the back of the van. "They're still walking out toward the fence. You have your company name splashed *all over* this damn thing, Fortuna. If you don't go any faster, they'll *know* it was us."

"You mean they'll know it was me," I muttered. I pushed my foot down on the gas and raised the speed to thirty-five. The van shot forward.

It was at that *very* moment a group of teenagers jumped out in front of my vehicle, and I heaved the steering wheel hard to the left. We missed the group by no more than an inch—but slammed the curb so hard the wheels rode up onto the grass to the right of the sidewalk. Pepper yelped. The Sprinter tilted so far over it seemed on the verge of toppling, but I gripped the steering wheel while simultaneously visualizing the four wheels stuck to the ground.

I was a witch. It might work.

I finally regained some measure of control and

brought the vehicle back down to the road past the teenagers.

"Are they still following?" I asked, checking the rearview mirror.

"No, I don't think so," Ollie said. "At least, I don't see any lights coming after us."

Pepper exhaled hard. "Well, that was exciting."

"And informative," Ollie said as they came back up to the front of the van and settled back in their seats. "Why would Mayor Saunders have two armed guards on her door?"

"Well, people are acting like crazy people," I pointed out. "Maybe she just hired some off-duty police officers to make sure her family was protected."

"After telling the doctor at Mystic's End Hospital not to worry about anything?" I glanced over and noticed Peppers's arms were crossed. "Whatever's going on in this town? The mayor has to know about it. No, more than that." Pepper slammed her palm down on the dashboard. "Mayor Saunders let it happen."

"Well, *that* just came out of left field," Ollie said.

"Can you think of any other reason Mayor Saunders would tell Dr. Arnhem not to worry about whatever this is? Especially when *she* was worried enough to have two big guys with big guns guarding her home?"

Pepper had a point.

When I first met Pepper Stanford, I thought she was interesting. I also thought she was a little bit of a loon. She seemed to see black helicopters, secret agents, and conspiracies around every corner. Though to be fair to her, she turned out to be right about a lot of things—there were witches. This town had a paranormal past corrupting its present. Statistically, women seem to die here at a rate that wasn't normal.

Some things she believed she had evidence for.

Some things she believed were just gut feelings that something was off.

Right now, we had no real evidence that Mayor Saunders was involved in whatever this happy-demic was. Considering what was going on in the town, a wealthy family hiring armed guards wasn't exactly a stretch to justify. Sure, you add in what she said to Dr. Arnhem, and it looks a *little* more suspicious.

Add in a limo she doesn't own? A little *more* suspicious.

Why would anyone infect the entire town, though? It made little sense.

On the other hand, I'd learned not to dismiss Pepper's gut reactions.

"Hey, Ollie, is Gideon okay back there?" I asked. "I haven't heard a peep out of him this whole time. The van got jostled pretty hard. Do you see him?"

"I see him. He's still sleeping."

"He *slept* through that?"

"Yep," Ollie told me cheerfully. "He must feel pretty safe around you. Greyhounds are pretty nervous dogs sometimes, and he's snoring away on his cushion."

* * *

We were turning into the parking lot at the track when a clunk echoed in the van.

"What the hell was that?" Pepper asked, her eyes wide.

Ollie pointed out the front window. "Your pet vampire."

Jeeves walked around toward the passenger side and pulled the door open. "I apologize if my landing on the roof frightened you. And, by the way, Oliver—if anyone is a pet here, it would be the other way—"

"Okay, okay, how about we not start this up again, huh?" I told Jeeves, cutting him off.

Pepper jumped out of the passenger seat and moved into the back of the van with Ollie as the vampire climbed in and took her place. "I knew it was you," she told the vampire confidently.

"You didn't," he responded just as confidently. "With time, your instincts might be better."

"With time?" Ollie stared at Jeeves, his eyes narrowing. "What do you mean 'with time'?"

"Your romantic partner has decided that she doesn't wish to give up the bond," Jeeves told him as we made our way around the various parking lots and toward the casino entrance. "As someone bonded to a vampire, she does get certain...perks. From what I can sense, she quite likes those perks."

"You got a lot to say for a reanimated corpse, you know," Ollie told him snidely. He turned around and walked to the back of the van and gazed out the window. I could hear him muttering things like *undead, post-human, bloodthirsty, heartless,* and *predatory.*

"He'll get used to it," Pepper told Jeeves. "Where have you been?"

"Don't you know?" Jeeves turned to look at Pepper, and I could feel the intensity of their connection like it was a wave being splashed all over me. Pepper's affection for Jeeves was through the roof. It was as if, in her eyes, he could do no wrong.

"Wow," I muttered, glancing at him. "*That's* really something."

"It comes in handy," the vampire responded with a slight smile.

"I imagine so. Especially for vampires that want to abuse people."

That wiped the smile right off his face. Ha.

"I went back to Grigio Hills to check on Martin. I sensed that he was..." Jeeves stopped himself, and his eyes flickered between us. "Well, in any case, I wanted to make sure that all was well. Addie, by the way, is beside herself with excitement that you can open a bottle."

"I know that you guys are hyper-focused on the bottle situation, but did you happen to find out anything about the happy-demic situation?"

"The *happy-demic*?" From the look Jeeves shot me, I could tell he thought little of my epidemic nickname. "You're calling what's happening here a happy-demic?"

"Well, I don't know what else to call it. Everyone gets real happy, overindulges on something that they really love, and then eventually they die. Happy-demic."

"At least we *think* they die," Pepper corrected. "So far, we don't know that anyone's died. Jeeves could be wrong about what he sensed in the blood."

"I beg your pardon?" Jeeves asked her, offended at the idea that he could be wrong about blood in any capacity. "I'm a vampire. If there's one thing I'm an expert on, it's blood."

"Yeah, well, I'm a witch, and most of the time, I don't think I know jack about magic."

I parked the van in one of the few open spots in front of the casino, and we climbed out. Gideon raced to follow.

"No, buddy." I turned. "People are acting nuts, and this isn't exactly the safest place for you. I don't want you to get kidnapped or caged up or something."

Gideon's head drooped and he whined.

"I'm sorry, Gid. This shouldn't take too long. We'll be back soon, I promise."

Gideon padded back to into the shadows of the van and sat down with a loud, put-upon sigh. I checked his water and food bowl, and closed the back door reluctantly. I hated leaving him in there alone, but I didn't want some crazed track worker snatching up my dog.

Again.

I'd been to the track before, and I didn't think I'd *ever* seen so many parking spots filled. Cars and trucks and buses were parked in every available space as far as the eye could see. Many were haphazardly stopped outside the lines. As we walked toward the casino, we could see numerous cars with their driver's door open. Many engines were still running. Several had even crashed into other vehicles.

"This is absolutely crazy," Ollie muttered. "I can't believe anyone would do this."

As we opened the door and walked inside, a cacophony of sounds assailed our ears.

SEVENTEEN

The warble of slot machines rotating, the slamming of hands on buttons, and people swearing. The air was filled with those three sounds. The closer we walked to the open archway that led into the casino, the more earsplitting it became.

The ceilings within were spotted with dome cameras that recorded everything that happened on the floor of the casino, and I made a mental note to go in search of the security room where they were kept. As my eyes took in the scene, I looked up, and my jaw dropped.

"This place is called *The Amber Chalice Casino?*" I asked Jeeves, surprised. "Is that new? The name, I mean. Did someone change it?"

"No," he said distractedly, scanning the casino floor. "Why?"

I didn't answer, but Mystic's End now had a *Golden Cup Coffee House*, and an *Amber Chalice Casino*. The odds of those names being so similar, and the odds of the two business being connected, were probably high. Or low. I frowned. Were high odds good or low odds good?

As you can tell, I'm not a gambler.

Or very good at math.

In any case, it made me even more suspicious of Dalida Dodd and her coffee—regardless of what the tests said. The two names couldn't be a coincidence.

The casino was filled with red-eyed, excited people pushing buttons on the brightly lit slot machines as if they were in some sort of trance. Every once in a while, a cheer would go up as a slot machine blared a win with all the urgency of a tornado siren. To the right, toward the table games, dozens of people were curled up on the green felt tables asleep. Clear plastic cups were strewn all over the floor, and a ribbon of smoke weaved its way through the colossal gambling hall.

"I don't see any security or waitresses," Jeeves said quietly.

"I do," Ollie told him, pointing to a waitress. "There's one on that slot machine."

"More than one," Pepper said, pointing to a few more people. "Everyone that works here is pumping cash into these machines just like the tourists."

"Okay, let's try and figure this out," I said, turning around to face Pepper. "When you came here on Friday morning, what did you do first?"

"I played this machine over here," Pepper said, picking her way through the glassy-eyed crowd. We —Jeeves, Ollie, and I—followed her until a strong hand grabbed my arm.

"Get down!" Jeeves hissed.

The four of us squatted down on the floor behind a large gaming machine with neon-colored fish all over it. Patrons stumbled around us as if we weren't even there.

"What is it?" I whispered.

"Don Salvatore," he whispered back. "I'm not supposed to be here, remember?"

I didn't remember.

Peeking around the machine, I saw Martin Salvatore walking in the hallway in front of the casino trailed by at least ten severe-looking women. He didn't look harried or glassy-eyed in the least bit.

"Who's that next to him?" Pepper hissed. "I can't see, he's blocking them."

"I think it's a woman," Ollie whispered back. "Though since all the people I can see are women, it's a pretty safe bet that one is, too."

Suddenly, Martin's father stopped, and the person beside him stepped forward.

It was Mystic's End mayor, Mirabelle Saunders.

The mayor's face was etched with worry, but she didn't look glassy-eyed or out of control. Her face was turned upward toward the handsome mafia godfather, her hands clutched in front of her as if pleading with him.

"Can you hear what they're saying?" Pepper whispered.

"I can't, but I bet Jeeves can," I whispered back.

"I can't," he answered through clenched teeth.

"Of course you can," I told him as he crouched next to me. "They're only twenty-five feet away from us. I've seen you eavesdrop across ten times that distance."

Jeeves's face twisted with a mix of anger and frustration. "You don't understand. I can't...tell you."

My head snapped around. "You *can* hear them, but you won't tell us what they're saying?"

Jeeves didn't answer.

Ollie gestured at the vampire, "I thought he said he would help us?"

"He did." I glared at Jeeves. "Apparently, that has its limits."

Jeeves turned toward me, his face twisted in

frustration. "I *told* you once there were lines I would not cross."

"Won't, or can't? Just how much magic is wrapped around you, vampire?" I asked him, referencing the witch magic the Dastardly Crime Family had placed on the vampire to make him more useful to them. "Are you making a choice here, or is this an obligation?"

"Does it matter?"

"Oh, yeah, it matters," I stood up and crossed my arms.

"Get down!" Jeeves hissed.

"I'm not hiding from anyone," I told him, shrugging. "This *is* a public place, right? I'm allowed to be here the same as anyone else." I turned toward the hallway to find Don Salvatore watching me. I waved. He nodded back. I turned and glared at Jeeves. "See? He doesn't have a problem with me, right?"

"You're going to get yourself *killed*," Jeeves warned me, still crouching.

"You didn't answer my question," I told him. "Are you not telling us what they said out there because you won't? Or because you can't?"

"I don't see the point—"

"There's a large group of people out there—witches, the mayor, Martin's dad—looking into this chaotic scene like they're checking on a pot of water boiling. They're clearly not affected by whatever this is, and since they're not affected, this scene *should* cause alarm. You know what I don't feel from them?"

Jeeves stared at me.

"Alarm?" Pepper guessed.

"Exactly. None of those things strike them as particularly odd. Well, not the mayor, anyway. I can't read anything off the Dreamboat Don thanks to the magical burrito your witches have him wrapped in. But nothing they see particularly freaks them out. Not the people sleeping on poker tables, the cups all over the floor, the lack of security. None of it. Mayor Saunders isn't surprised at all." I glared down at the vampire. "And I think *you* know why."

Jeeves was hunched forward, his shoulders knotted tensely—as if he carried a great weight on them. His eyes, though, were cold, and he didn't answer.

"You're not really going to help us, are you?" Ollie asked finally.

"There are things I can't do and lines I can't cross—"

"Your loyalty is admirable. Really," I told the vampire in a tone of voice that communicated unmistakably that I didn't find it all that admirable. "It's a shame that hundreds of people may die for your vampiric version of morality, but I guess that's the way things are sometimes, right?"

I turned on my heel and headed straight toward the mayor.

"Fortuna!" Jeeves hissed.

I ignored him.

* * *

"Ms. Delphi," Don Salvatore called as I walked out of the casino and into the gigantic hallway of the racetrack. "Pleasure to see you again. Mayor Saunders, I'm sure you know Ms. Delphi." He swept his arm gallantly from the nervous mayor over to me. "She owns an art business in the center of town."

"No, I don't know her," Mayor Saunders answered nervously in a high-pitched squeak. The well-dressed woman gnawed at a fingernail as her eyes bounced back and forth between us. "I don't get out much, you know. I like to stay in my house."

This was the mayor? With her mousy personality, she would have trouble keeping control of an animated PTA meeting, much less this town.

"Mayor, what's going to be done about all this?" I asked, waving behind me.

"About all what?" she asked, gnawing harder at the nail, her eyes moving quickly back and forth.

She looked like a squirrel keeping an eye out for a cat about to pounce.

"The whole town seems to have gone a little crazy. Haven't you noticed?" I raised an eyebrow.

The phalanx of women behind the mayor and the mafia don stared at me, eyes narrowed. Their muscles twitched, and beads of sweat gathered on their brows as they, I suspected, tried to read my mind. I thanked Samson again for the small stone stuck in my bra that kept their efforts from bothering me in the least.

"I don't know what you mean," the mayor whispered. Her eyes skipped over to Don Salvatore, and then back to the ground. "It's the holidays, people are just having fun."

Behind me, an older man collapsed to the ground. Coins exploded in all directions as his cup slammed to the floor. In a mad scramble, casino patrons dove to gather up the money in their hands like zombies that had found a pond of brain matter. With their eyes alight, they turned and raced back into the casino, leaving the man snoring on the floor.

"Does that look like fun to you?" I asked her. Without waiting for her to respond, I turned toward the Don. "Where's Martin? His employees are affected by whatever this thing is that's got the town in its grips. I would think that presents a security risk for someplace like a casino, don't you think?"

"There's no risk to anyone here," he told me pleasantly. The phalanx of women behind him nodded. He did not tell me where Martin was.

I could sense nothing from anyone in that hallway despite my best efforts. Martin Salvatore was unreadable. The women, too. It was as if they weren't even standing in front of me. Every one of them was just blank. Blank expressions, blank emotions, expressionless eyes.

Well, not Don Salvatore. His expression was dismissive, but his gaze searched my face as if looking for something he couldn't quite find.

"Well, there must be *some* risk to people here. The Mayor has two armed guards at her house," I disagreed. "Why would there be guards at her house if there was no threat to the house or the people in it?"

No one responded to my question.

The mayor's nervousness, Martin Salvatore's nonchalant calm, and Jeeves's inability to tell me what the two spoke about—they all set my suspicions into overdrive. I knew, without a doubt, that Don Salvatore's arrival in Mystic's End was responsible for what was happening to the town.

I had no proof, but I knew. Too many things led back to him.

"If you'll excuse us, Miss Delphi, we have other things to attend to." Don Salvatore bowed his head slightly and gave me a half-smile. "I'm sure we'll see each other again before I leave town." He turned and stared viciously at the women behind him. "Let's go."

I watched the twelve walk away toward the administrative buildings.

* * *

"Sit down," I ordered Jeeves, pointing to a chair at the empty casino bar.

To my surprise, Jeeves sat.

"I talked to Uncle Vito when we went to Mystic Memories Senior Living Center." I pulled out a chair and sat down in front of him. Ollie and Pepper watched with interest. "He told me two things were going on with Salvatore. One, he wanted Martin to know he was still in control. Two, he wanted to know what Martin wasn't telling him."

Jeeves stared back.

"And by the way, Uncle Vito told me that Martin's father knows about the bottles—and he also told me that the Don never told Martin."

Jeeves' jaw dropped.

"So why don't you start talking?"

"He can't," Pepper burst out, her eyes wide. "He can't tell you. I don't know if he wants to tell you or doesn't, but I know somehow that he literally can't. Like, he can't *say* the words. I don't know if it's a vampire thing or a witch magic thing or what it is, but I can feel it. He just can't."

"Is that true?" I asked the vampire.

Jeeves glanced away.

"You are the single most frustrating human being I've ever dealt with!" I shouted in frustration.

Pepper held up a finger. "So, you know, he's not a human—"

"I know he's not a human being!" I shouted even louder, my fists balled. "No one can be this controlled by magic! It's just not *possible*. You can't override someone's will this long, this hard, and this completely. He's either completely full of it and a liar or—"

"Maybe it's not just magic," Ollie said quietly, staring at Jeeves.

"What do you mean, hon?" Pepper turned and looked at Ollie. "Fortuna could see it. That he was wrapped in magical shields and stuff that kept her from reading him."

"She's right, though. I studied magic with the coven in Austin. Controlling other people is, like, huge magic," Ollie said, moving in and lowering his voice. "She's lived at one of the circuses. They could make pockets of time and space, but they couldn't control other witches, other paranormals.

That's literally the whole reason the circuses came to be. Rebellious paranormals that didn't want to live by the Council rules, right?" Ollie looked at me.

"Yeah, as far as I know." I thought back to the circus, whether I'd seen anyone controlled by someone else, and I couldn't think of a single instance that went on longer than an hour. And it was never this complete. "So, what are you saying?"

"Let's accept Pepper's assertion that he is being controlled to an extent. At least on some things," Ollie said, pacing. "If it's not magic, what could be doing it?"

I snapped my head up. "Blood. Vampires were absolutely, positively, never allowed at the circuses, ever. In fact, everyone was afraid of them. Like, *really* afraid."

"Maybe they were afraid because vampires could make them walk out of the circus boundaries whether they wanted to or not," Ollie said as he turned to look at Jeeves. "Can you tell us if we're right?" Ollie paused as Jeeves shifted uncomfortably. "Or is even that freedom taken from you, too?"

Jeeves's gaze shot daggers at Ollie.

"Well, he's not leaving, so that's a good sign," Pepper said cheerfully.

"But he's not talking," I pointed out.

The vampire stared into my eyes. "There's nothing I can say to you."

"But if you weren't hiding anything, you could tell us we were wrong," I said softly. "Are we wrong?"

Jeeves, caught between whatever he was bound to and me, said nothing.

I tilted my head. "Not a slave, huh?"

The vampire winced.

EIGHTEEN

"Fortuna, wait," Jeeves said as I walked toward the free drink area. All this running around had made me thirsty. "Calm down and let me explain."

I whirled to face him. "First of all, don't tell me to calm down. Just because I'm aggravated with your lies and don't trust you doesn't mean that I'm overly emotional. It's insulting."

Jeeves stared at me, seemingly unperturbed. "It was not my intention to insult you."

"Oh, shut up already, will you?" I turned on my heel and continued my walk toward the drink station. In Las Vegas, waitresses would bring gamblers free drinks to keep them at the slot machines or the tables. This, though, wasn't Vegas.

In Mystic's End, gamblers got up to get their *own* free soda, and the waitresses concentrated on serving cheap but profitable alcoholic beverages. "I can't believe anything you say anymore."

"I've never lied to you," Jeeves argued.

"So, there are two ways people can deceive other people, right?" I grabbed a paper cup and thrust it into the ice machine. With a whir, the lever brought the machine to life, and ice dropped into my cup. "One is that you can tell them an outright lie. You move your lips, say words that aren't true." Once the cup was filled, I glanced at the soda offerings and picked lemon-lime. "The other way is to know something they need to know and not tell them. Or simply not answer. Not speak up when they need an answer you know." I turned, holding my drink, and stared at Jeeves. "You probably lie to me all the time. It's just that they're lies of omission."

I brought the cup to my lips, and Jeeves reached out and slapped it—hard—from my hand. It went flying into the side of a slot machine. Ice and liquid went everywhere.

"Well, that was certainly unexpected." I stared at the vampire, his face still impassive, and fought the urge to slap *him*. "What did you do that for?"

Jeeves stared at me and said nothing.

I eyed the soda machine and glanced at the

plastic cups strewn over the floor. People had been drinking a lot of soda from the machines. While I watched, another gambler raced over, refilled his plastic cup with cola, and ran off while gulping it down. "You don't want me to drink the soda," I murmured, glancing back at him. "Why don't you want me to drink that?"

More impassive staring from Sparkles. But no answers.

"You *can't* tell me, can you?" I said out loud. I looked at the vampire deep into his eyes. If there was a desire, a want, an opinion? I couldn't see it. "But you didn't want me to drink that. Why wouldn't you want me to drink that?" I tilted my head. "Have you known what's causing this the *whole* time?"

Jeeves was immobile, and he stared at me with all the emotion of the statue.

"Pepper, Ollie!" I called over the casino cacophony. "Come here!"

Seconds later, the two popped out from behind the video poker machines.

"Sparkles over here just whacked a cup out of my hand before I could drink my soda," I told them, my finger pointing to Jeeves's center of mass. "He didn't say anything before doing it and won't say anything to me about why he did it now." I turned to Pepper. "Did you have anything from the drink station when you came to the casino, Pepper?"

"I think so," she said, tilting her head. "I mean, usually do. I can't remember specifically whether I did that morning, but I drink cola and coffee in the morning sometimes. So, it sounds like something I would do."

"I wasn't drinking cola," I murmured, glancing at all of the offerings. I turned toward the vampire and considered what he hadn't said and what he'd done. "Why can you keep me from drinking from the fountain, but not answer me?"

More staring.

Suddenly, I gasped.

"Martin made you swear to protect me. You can't let anything happen to me. That's what this is, isn't it? You're caught between two directives, like a robot that has conflicting programming," I guessed. "One, Martin told you not to let anything happen to me, and you know that something at the drink station could threaten me. Two," I told him, stepping closer. "Two, your mafia masters did something to this town, and you know what it is. But you're bound or oathed or sworn or magicked to not expose them. Am I close?"

Jeeves glanced away toward the door and then back down to me. His nostrils flared as if he was breathing heavily.

"Nothing to say?" I turned and grabbed another cup. "Well, I think we can figure this out without you saying a word, Sparkles." I got myself some coffee, black, and slowly brought it to my lips. Jeeves didn't make a move as I swallowed. "Just to make sure you're still gonna save me," I said, getting myself another lemon-lime soda. When the cup was halfway to my mouth, Jeeves's slapped it from my hand again.

"I don't get it, what does that prove?" Ollie asked.

"She's going to test different theories," Pepper told him, pointing. "There's nothing in the coffee that will harm her, so he let her drink it. There's something in the lemon-lime soda that will hurt her, and so he couldn't let her drink that." Pepper turned to me. "So, it's not in the water itself."

"No, it's not in the water," I agreed and glanced at the vampire. "So, is it the syrup? The ice? The carbonation?"

Again, no response.

"Aw, Jeeves, you're making this a game, you know that?" I grabbed another cup, filled it with ice, and brought it to my lips—no concern and no movement from Sparkles. I dumped the ice cubes in my mouth and chewed.

"Ew, I hate when people chew ice." Ollie shuddered. "It sounds like bones breaking."

"The guy that works with dead people doesn't like ice chewing?" Pepper asked, her eyebrow raised.

"Everyone has their things, you know?"

"Okay, it's not the ice, it's not the water," I told him as I tossed away the cup and grabbed another. I looked at the variety of flavors and went for the cola without ice. I pulled the cup toward my lips, and Jeeves smacked from my hand. "Okay, it's not the syrup."

"It could be both syrups," Ollie pointed out. "Maybe that shipment of syrups was contaminated with something. I just don't think we should rule it out."

"We can rule it out pretty easily, though. You see that one under the lemon-lime? The black bar marked water?" Pepper pointed. "That's not just water, but soda water. Carbonated water without any syrup whatsoever."

"Okay, trying that one," I said once more, and filled up the cup.

Jeeves never allowed it to get close to my lips.

"It's the carbonation," the three of us said in unison.

* * *

"How much soda do people drink in this town?" Pepper asked as we opened up the cabinets below the drink station and unhooked the carbonation canisters. "I mean, are all the carbonated drinks in the whole track laced with something?"

"The entrances to the casino are designed to funnel people in, to catch people's attention as they walk by going to different places in the complex," Ollie called from underneath the counter. "No matter where you go in this track, at *some* point, you're going to walk in front of one of the casino entrances."

"And everywhere else, you have to pay top dollar for a soda. Here?" Pepper pointed to the big archway that opened up to the path that went around the greyhound track. "You can see the gigantic free soda sign, just walking by. If I had to guess, that's deliberate. It's a way to get people in here in hopes they'll gamble their money away."

"Why else have a casino with no doors?" Ollie added.

"The other carbonated soda places might be laced with whatever is making people turn into nut jobs, but you also have to remember the casino is owned by Martin's company," Pepper said as Ollie passed her a canister. "A lot of those places out there—the restaurants, the food court—are leased spots. Companies that run 'em? They're owned by other people. Not Martin's family. They'd likely do their own purchasing."

"The casino is owned by Martin's father," Jeeves burst out.

"He speaks," I mumbled as Ollie and I rolled the canister away from the drink station and examined it. "Thanks for your contribution, Jeeves. Super helpful. Really."

I was incredibly frustrated with the vampire. I spent months being wary of trusting Martin and Jeeves, and I went back and forth pretty frequently on whether to help them. The simple fact was we were both after the same thing—the witch bottles— and that made us allies of a sort. But a part of me felt I was in some *Jason Bourne* ripoff where nothing was what it seemed, and everybody was keeping secrets.

Most of the time, the secret-keeping was *just* annoying.

This time, it was dangerous.

"Actually, Sparkles might have a good point," Pepper said as she examined the canister for markings. "If Don Salvatore owns this place outright—wait a minute," Pepper turned toward Jeeves. "He's a known gangster. How on earth could that man get a license to own a gambling establishment? There's *no* way."

"It can be done quite easily. Any rule or law can be worked around," Jeeves responded, shrugging. "Shell corporations, patsy puppet owners. It's quite simple and done often."

"By you people, maybe," I said. "The rest of us out here? We try and follow the rules, not look for ways around them so we can get what we want."

"Okay, I looked at every inch of this carbonation thing. There's nothing about this canister that looks out of the ordinary except for one thing," Pepper said. "There's no company name on here at all. No canister number, no company name, no identifying marks."

"Why is that odd?" I asked her.

"Because carbon dioxide comes in these cylinders, right? The soda machines don't pump out soda. They run water through the carbonation process and then mix in the syrup at the last second to give you the soda that you want. That's how those fountains work." Pepper reached down and leaned the canister up. "So, they're huge, but at some point, these canisters are going to run out of carbon dioxide. The company is gonna bring a new full canister and take the old one to refill it. That's why they usually have company names and numbers on them. So the carbonation place can keep track of who has what canister and when it needs to be replaced."

"But that's not on there?"

"No. These have no scratches on them, no wear on them." Pepper leaned it back. "It's like they're brand spanking new and completely unmarked."

"Okay, then let's check all of the carbonation stations. We can unhook any that look brand-new and have no identifying marks," I told them. "Once we fix the situation here, we can check the other places selling soda nearby. If none of those have these canisters, it seems reasonable to assume it's just the casino."

"We know *what* seems to be doing it, but we don't know who," Ollie said.

"Or how, or why," Pepper added.

"That's why we need to find the security monitoring place where they keep the footage." I pointed to the dark domed bubbles every five feet along the ceiling. "Every inch of this place is under surveillance. We just need to figure out who put those canisters in. Then we'll have the proof."

"What are we going to do with them?" Pepper asked.

I smiled. "I have an idea. Let's just store them for now. Someplace Don Salvatore won't know to look."

* * *

W e split up.

Ollie found a flat dolly to use so he and Pepper could collect the CO_2 canisters. Jeeves knew where the security booth was located—and seemed to have his magical leash loosened enough he agreed to show me where it was.

"I can't believe you confronted Don Salvatore after I specifically asked you to stay out of his awareness," Jeeves said as we picked our way through the revelers.

"I can't believe I thought your silence when we first met was deep and sexy, but it was really just you being unable to utter a single word to anyone without your mafia master's permission," I responded with a sarcastic smile. "*Why* did you even agree to help us when you already knew what was going on, and you knew you weren't really going to be able to help us?"

"I have helped as much as I could—I have competing loyalties." Jeeves stopped and turned. "Wait, you thought I was sexy?"

I walked past him rolling my eyes. "Shut up. Are any of those choices? The competing loyalties thing?"

He pushed past me and walked faster. "We all make choices."

"Some of us clearly less than others," I said, following him in a door marked *Security*. Once the door smacked shut behind me, the vampire whirled on me in the darkened hall with a speed that made me jump. He spread his arms out, so his palms rested on both sides of the narrow corridor and stared down at me. "What? What now?"

"I risked my immortality to come when you called," Jeeves said, his voice low. "Our lives have collided here in this place, at this time. I could have refused to help your friend Pepper, but I did not. I risked myself to help her. To help you."

"What do you want, a medal?" I snapped. "People could die from this. Did you know that before you took a sip of Pepper? Did you know that after the property damage, the monetary damage, the crazy behavior, people could *die*?"

He frowned. "No, I didn't—"

"Oh, you *didn't*?" I shouted, feigning surprise. "Of course you didn't! You *say* you didn't, so of course you didn't! And yet—how am I supposed to believe you now that I know you're so wrapped up in your stupid oaths and obligations to criminals that you may not be telling me the truth at all!"

"I told you I would never lie to you—"

I put my hands on my hips and thrust my chin out. "And I have *no* way to know whether that's even the truth. Do I?"

"Well, you *do*," the vampire said, smiling like

the cat that ate the canary. "But you wouldn't like it."

The sound that a vampire's teeth make when they extend? It's kind of like a sword unsheathing. Two tiny swords that glint menacingly even in the dimmest of hallways.

NINETEEN

We stared at one another so long, I could feel my cheeks flushing hot in the cold corridor.

"Has this been your plan all along?" I asked him as his sharp eyes peered deeply into mine. My eyelids felt heavy in the dark coolness as if I was in some trance, and I tried to remember the last time I slept. "Get me into a situation where having a vampiric tie to you might be beneficial and whip out the chompers?"

"First, my incisors do not chomp, they pierce. Second, no," Jeeves answered simply.

More silence.

Even though I'd known the vampire for months, he was still a mystery. Jeeves was hard to read, his passive face betraying nothing about what he might feel or think most of the time. With the possible exception of when we were back in that circle, and he was wrapped in a psychic Hecatoncheires costume.

Greek mythology? The hundred-handed ones? Anyway.

Sparkles was still a mystery to me.

"How did Martin get you to agree to this?" I asked him point-blank. "How on earth did you decide to become what you are *willingly*? You're not even just a vampire. You're a vampire programmed and forced to bow to someone else's wishes, morals, desires. How can that *not* bother you?" I asked him seriously. "How can you *live* like this?"

"Are you concerned for my *feelings*, Fortuna?" Jeeves asked, his voice light with barely suppressed amusement. I wanted to smack him for making fun of me.

"I'm serious," I said, poking him in the chest. "You know, it's hard to periodically like someone and then be worried that they're just jerking you around for someone else's agenda."

His fangs withdrew, and he moved closer. "I know you are serious," Jeeves murmured, his face growing anxious as he read distress in my eyes. "I wish I knew what to say that would help you to realize you can trust me." He tilted his head. "Your heart is beating so quickly. Please don't be apprehensive or frightened. I told you once that you are just as much of a threat to me as I am to you. We have mutually assured destruction keeping us both at bay."

"I'm not nervous," I explained to him.

"Of course."

"Or frightened!" I added hotly.

Silence.

He was right. My heart was beating quickly because I was in a quiet, concrete-encased hallway with a vampire that had just expressed an interest in biting me.

But it was also because the vampire was incredibly close.

And incredibly handsome.

I took a step back.

It was just his stupid vampire glamour powers. It had to be. They were probably more potent in an enclosed space than they were usually.

Maybe.

"I'm not talking about survival here, Jeeves—and *why* am I calling you Jeeves? Even that's just ridiculous. Martin wanted to change your name, so you just let him change your name?"

"Why does my lack of autonomy so concern you?" He was half-smiling, as if my concern for his servitude was adorable and quaint. "I told you before, it was my decision. I am not like the greyhounds at this track that have no choice in the matter regarding who their careers benefit. I made a choice to become what I am, and I was handsomely rewarded for it."

"How?" I asked again. "Why did you make this choice? Why are you doing what you're doing?" I stepped closer to the vampire and looked up into his eyes, pleading with him. "How could anyone make a choice to become what you are? To be what you are?"

"You want to count on me," Jeeves observed. Then he nodded with an expression that might have been satisfaction. "I need that trust to find Martin's mother. I'll make a deal with you."

"What kind of deal?" I asked suspiciously.

"Once we save the town from the scourge of carbonation," Jeeves said, turning and glancing at the door marked *Security* at the opposite end of the hall, "and before you open the two remaining bottles at your home, I will tell you the story of how I came to be Martin's bonded vampire. And you can judge my motives if you wish."

"I'll settle for knowing your motives." I thought about it for a moment and then nodded. I would have opened the bottles anyway, but he didn't need to know that. "I don't want to judge you, Jeeves—"

"You don't know yourself very well, do you?" he asked me. Without waiting for an answer, he turned and walked toward the security room.

* * *

The wall of screens on the north end of the room gave us a clear view of almost every aspect of the track: the kennels, the hallways, the front facades of the various shops and restaurants. I blushed hotly as I glanced at the screen showing the strip club.

"Not too much destruction, at least," Jeeves observed, taking in the scene. "Martin will be pleased about that. Just a lot of trash. The cleaning crew will be busy for a day or so." He walked around the enormous room and checked behind file cabinets and under desks.

If Martin had a large security force, they were *nowhere* to be seen.

The center of all surveillance at the track was a vast gray room with no windows and dozens of flickering screens covering one full wall. About a dozen desks with office chairs and computers were arranged as if the room was an amphitheater and the screens were the show. I moved to one of the counters on the top level and looked at the papers strewn about on it.

"I suppose the guards like free soda," I said as I picked up a plastic casino cup.

"Lock the door, would you?" Jeeves called from three desk-rows down, gesturing back toward the one door in or out of the place. "I'd prefer to do this undisturbed by rabble-rousers."

I locked the exit. "I guess no one's obsessed with their job."

"Most people aren't, I suppose. Just give me a moment, and I'll pull up the footage." The loud clickety-clack of the keyboard echoed in the room. Within seconds, the entire wall of screens went black and was replaced by a massive image of the drink station. "When was Pepper at the casino?"

"Black Friday morning," I called down.

"Let's start at midnight. I can speed it up, so we don't have to sit through hours of film."

People began rapidly moving in and out of the frame as the vampire and I watched.

Two, three, four in the morning. Janitors came and went, cleaning the station. Many people—far more than I would have thought—came up to the station to get caffeinated beverages in the middle of the night on Thanksgiving. Presumably, so they could fuel their gambling binge.

Finally, at six in the morning, a young woman with long blonde hair stepped in front of the station. She raised her arms, and a flash of light nearly blinded me. I rubbed my eyes and blinked a few times to get the sparkling dots out from my vision. When I looked back at the screen, she was gone.

"What the heck was that?" I asked the vampire.

"Clarissa," Jeeves said as if that was an explanation. "That was Clarissa."

"And Clarissa is?"

"A witch. A relatively new one, actually." Jeeves punched a few more buttons and brought the multiple vantage points back up. "I think she joined the brigade about six months ago." I was pretty proud of myself when I didn't roll my eyes at the mention of "the brigade." Turning, he looked up at me. "This must be her graduation act."

"Her *what* now?"

"The first six months in the brigade, witches are trained. Given powers, bound to oaths, wrapped in magic," the vampire said as he walked up the stairs to join me. His face had that *I'm not sure if I should be telling you* this expression, but since no magic popped up and stuck a sock in his mouth, I guess he felt it was safe to continue. "On a paranormal's six month anniversary, they have to perform an operation that benefits the family."

A thing that benefits the family? This whole thing was continuing its slow slide toward an unquestionably bad eighties movie. "The witch family," I guessed.

Jeeves shook his head no. "Martin's family."

"So, Don Salvatore told her to do this."

Jeeves shook his head no. "No one *tells* you what to do. It's like a final test, the last step before you fully join the family." I nodded as if I understood, but I wasn't sure I did. Jeeves seemed to sense that, so he continued. "The clan doesn't want—as you so offensively keep putting it—slaves that do nothing more than what they're told. They want paranormals that can think creatively. People that can put things into action while understanding the potential consequences. Using their powers."

"So, to prove that you can do that, you guys come up with some big, beneficial gesture that helps the family?" Jeeves nodded. "And you assume that might be this?" Jeeves nodded again. "You have security guards snoring on the roulette table. How would this catastrophe benefit—"

I stopped myself and stared at the wall of screens flickering. People gathered around the slot machines and hit the button over, and over, and over. They pushed one another out of their way as they fought for prime positions on the highest limit slot machines.

I thought back to the woman in my shop, desperate to spend money. The paintings that flew out the door as if they'd grown wings. "It's about *money*," I said with a hard edge to my voice. "Clarissa put something in the CO_2 canisters so the patrons would spend as much money as possible at the casino. You said Don Salvatore owns it—this was her thing. She was trying to impress him by concocting something that would make them spend money. Only it didn't wind up being limited to money, or the casino. It spread throughout the town."

"It's possible," Jeeves admitted. "That *sounds* like something Clarissa would do." Jeeves's face dropped, and he suddenly looked angry. "And like something she would screw up."

"Why's that?"

"All of the witches—other than one—are partial witches," Jeeves explained, shifting uncomfortably. "Don Salvatore only has one full witch in the brigade. She may be just one, but she's quite powerful." Jeeves tried to smile, but he ended up just looking unhappy. "She controls us all in big and small ways. Just like I have some unique powers, it's the same for the half-witches."

I stared at Jeeves, astounded that he had just told me this.

I thought of Martin's family power and their sick infatuation with the paranormal world as a tool for crime. All of the paranormals they controlled, the humans they turned into foot soldiers. The damage they caused. They got away with it because of one specific person.

One single witch.

As the shock coursed through me, I did my best to keep my face expressionless. I didn't know how Jeeves was able to tell me what he told me, but I didn't want to do anything to zip his lip. "Okay, so why does that mean Clarissa would screw this up?"

"Clarissa is the Witch Queen's daughter," Jeeves explained. "She's young, barely eighteen, and she's...well, a bit spoiled. When she does make a mistake, it's not like anyone would have the bravery to tell her. She'd just run to her mother and, well..." Jeeves shrugged.

"Who's the Witch Queen?" I asked with a cheerful nonchalance.

Jeeves stared, his mouth closed, and his eyes hardened.

"There we are," I said, patting him on the shoulder. I cocked one eyebrow up. "I knew I'd hit that wall sooner or later. Come on, Sparkles. Let's go find the Witch Queen's daughter."

"But she's probably with Don Salvatore!" Jeeves said, growing alarmed.

"I won't say anything about the witch bottles, I promise," I told him, walking toward the door, my head held high. "Or the so-called 'Witch Queen.'

But this town is not a paranormal playground for your boss. Clarissa's graduation project came close to killing everyone in this town that likes a free soda, and your boss needs to make sure his pet witches don't go off the leash again."

Jeeves followed me reluctantly as I marched out of the security room to confront the mafia boss, the half-witches brigade, and the mayor—who I was pretty sure had let this all happen.

TWENTY

We caught up with Don Salvatore and his posse in the vast, winding passageway that wrapped around the greyhound track spectator stands. They were strolling and discussing the food booths, restaurants, and shops on the outer ring as if he was a president coming to examine a natural disaster.

"Mr. Salvatore, sir," I called out, Jeeves trailing behind me.

The group of women swung their heads to stare at me as if they were a parliament of owls.

Martin's father finished whatever he was saying to Mayor Saunders and then casually turned around to meet my approach with his gaze. "Mayor Saunders," I nodded to the woman politely and then dismissed her just as quickly—I knew who was calling the shots here, and I would not waste time with someone who wasn't.

"Miss Delphi, we're very busy—"

"Mr. Salvatore, if you were walking any more slowly around this track, you'd be standing still," I told him, and then glanced behind him at the women staring back at me. Nearly all were straight-backed and attentive. Suspicious, even. One young blonde, however, was twirling her hair and giggling as we spoke. "Is that Clarissa?" I asked him, pointing.

Jeeves tensed, and his ultimate boss frowned.

"What's the meaning of this?" Don Salvatore asked the vampire, ignoring my question.

Jeeves didn't respond.

Like, for a *long* time.

We waited, all staring at him.

But nope. Nothing.

Was he bound by Martin's requests and demands just as strongly as whatever allegiant magic the Witch Queen of the Dastardly Crime Family had cast? I examined his face for the telltale struggle as he fought his programming, and I saw hints of it. I suspected he was—but Don Salvatore clearly had no clue why one of his foot soldiers was staring at him and not answering.

"Jeeves, is it her?" I inquired again.

"Young lady, are you sure you know who I am?" Don Salvatore asked me, turning with a menacing expression on his face. When he stepped closer to me, his paranormal harem stepped closer to him as if they were attached. "Are you sure, very sure, you know who and what you're dealing with?"

"That's not the question, though, is it?" I raised my chin and walked closer. "The question is whether you know who *I* am. It's what you came here to figure out, right?" I paused. "So, did you? Figure out who I am, I mean?"

He looked down at me with an impassive expression. Still, I could see the surprise in his eyes I dared to challenge him so openly.

I honestly don't know where I got the fearlessness, or why my instincts told me I needed to cross swords with Martin's father. But I *had* the bravery. I was practically oozing bravado.

I also had unquestionable confidence in my urge to throw down the gauntlet. I knew, somehow, that running from him or hiding from him wasn't an option.

As we stared at one another, I could see *it* slowly come into focus...a silver cord. It was thin, like a delicate silver necklace. It stretched taut to my right. I turned my head slightly, following its path with my eyes—straight to Jeeves.

Unlike when we were in the circle, I could only see one.

That one tie. That one cord. That one connection.

Glancing around, I could also tell that no one else could see it.

Just me.

Visus, my mind called up the memory of Miss Bessie explaining my mystic power—a power that would just pop up out of nowhere to show me things. *It is the knowing that the mystic gets when face to face with wrong. It's a sixth sense—a knowing —that something is not what it appears to be to everybody else. It's not mind reading, just...a sense. An understanding, a recognition that something, or someone, is not as it appears. The wider the divergence between what we see and what is real, the sharper the visus.*

What was that last thing she said about it?

Oh, right.

It's just an arrow, dear, pointing you toward a path.

An arrow I was supposed to trust.

So I did.

And I reached out and cut the cord.

* * *

D on Salvatore didn't feel it, but Jeeves *sure* did. The mafia don's evil smile suddenly collapsed into watchful shock as his phalanx of witches surrounded him in a protective semi-circle. The entire group stared at Jeeves who dropped to his knees, heaving air through his lungs. He gasped and sputtered like a human who had just broken through the water's surface.

The half-witches looked furious.

And frightened.

"Is that man okay?" Mayor Saunders whimpered while pointing at Jeeves.

"Who are you?" Martin's father spat at me. "What did you just do?"

I shrugged. "He's no longer linked to you."

Don Salvatore's eyes widened. "You have joined him to you, then, witch?"

"So, is that a pejorative, or are you starting to clue in to what's going on here?" I asked with a smirk. My face hardened again. "I haven't tied him to anyone. I just removed his forced devotion to you."

"You *are* the mystic!" he growled. The tall man was struggling to pull himself from the arms of his women, but they held him fast, their eyes wide with fear. "I *knew* Martin was keeping a secret from me. You! It was you!"

I didn't know what, specifically, was me, but

apparently, I'd done something the Don knew about that he wasn't happy with.

"So, I, um, think I should go, maybe, and let you two talk," Mirabelle Saunders whispered, slowly slipping away from the group. "You seem to have a lot to talk about that I, um, maybe shouldn't be a part of. Maybe." One witch reached out and grasped her wrist, keeping her from moving away. The mayor cried out in shock, her body going tense.

"I can't read her," another witch said, focusing on me.

"I can't, either," yet another murmured.

"She's like a blank slate. *How* can that be?" a third asked, alarmed.

"Oh, man, my mom is going to be so annoyed with you guys," Clarissa sneered.

"Well, can *you* read her?" the first witch asked angrily.

"Please, let me just go home," Mayor Saunders whimpered.

Suddenly, out of nowhere, Miss Bessie and Mary Wilcox, Gabe's mother, poofed into view. Miss Bessie gave me a small, reluctant smile and nodded approvingly while Mary continued to stare at me with suspicion.

"Where have you all been?" I asked them.

"Who's she talking to?" the first witch asked. Several other half-witches mumbled that they didn't know as they swiveled their heads around on their necks.

"I wasn't going to let Gabe run into the woods by the reservoir with Clutterbuck all on his own. Obviously," Miss Bessie answered. Looking Jeeves up and down, she raised an eyebrow. "What's wrong with him?" The poor vampire was still coughing and looked alarmingly pale.

Well, more pale than usual.

"I cut the tie between Jeeves and Don Salvatore."

"Well, *that* was a bit ballsy, don't you think?" Mary asked wryly.

"Did you find out who poisoned the town?" Miss Bessie said before I could give a proper retort.

"Clarissa poisoned the town," I pointed to the now frowning blonde. "She put something in the carbonation, it got into the free sodas, and anyone in town that drank them got infected with something."

"I didn't poison the town, you moron!" Clarissa protested hotly. "I just added some probiotics to the drink. Probiotics are good for people! These just had a few little magical *tweaks* to help Don Salvatore make the money he needed to buy the penthouse in Las Vegas." She rocked back and forth on her heels, her hands held out. Clarissa's expression made it clear she was proud of herself.

"Everyone was just super happy. What's so bad about that?"

Jeeves groaned as if in pain, but then thrust himself up, his finger pointed at Clarissa. "Your *tweaks* caused your magical bacteria to colonize people at a rate their bodies couldn't fight," Jeeves told her, breathing heavily. He stepped up beside me and glared at the girl. "It jumped from their gut microbiome into their bloodstream and grew out of control!"

"What's a gut microbiome?" the girl asked, confused.

"You are an idiot!" Jeeves growled at her. The witches yelped and huddled together behind Don Salvatore—who was staring at his vampire in shock. "Why would you mess with things you have no understanding of? You put everyone at risk! What if Martin had drunk your concoction and become ill!"

"Well, of course, I kept my son away from the track while Clarissa performed her final test before formally joining the family," Don Salvatore told Jeeves, his voice threaded through with a menacing edge of derision. "Jeeves, I would suggest you get your anger and your disrespect under control. You may find the consequences more than you're willing to suffer through."

"That sounds like a terroristic threat to me." Chief Clutterbuck and Gabe stepped up to the group. "Mr. Salvatore, sir, I'm sure you don't want to do anything criminal. You know, to add to the already illegal things your girl over there did."

Don Salvatore smiled widely. "Chief, I'm so glad to see you—"

"I don't think you are," Chief Clutterbuck cut him off and pulled out handcuffs. Turning his gaze toward Clarissa, he held them out. "Are we going to do this the peaceful way, Miss, or the hard way? I've been up a long time, and it's been a pretty crappy day, so I'd prefer the easy way. But I'm sure Gabe here would be happy to help me out if things go sideways real fast."

"You *can't* be serious!" Don Salvatore shouted.

Chief Clutterbuck turned to him as Gabe took up a position behind a now panicked Clarissa. "Your girl poisoned my daughter."

The two men stared.

Clutterbuck said nothing else.

He didn't have to.

"Chief, I'm sure we can come to some sort of—"

"We *had* one of your arrangements," the chief declared, cutting Salvatore off. "One of the conditions *you* committed to was the safety of the people in this town—most especially my girl. *You* broke that." Turning to Mayor Saunders, he added, "And so did you. I'm like any other greedy country boy. I'll look the other way for a price up to a point."

He turned back to Don Salvatore. "You reached that end when my girl took your poison."

"It was just a probiotic!" Clarissa shouted as Clutterbuck walked toward her. With a small assist from Gabe, the two men had her in handcuffs. "If you don't let me go right now, I'm going to tell—"

Jeeves swooped in and gathered her in his arms before any of us blinked twice. With a few whispered words that no one could quite make out, the girl's eyes became unfocused, and she swayed on her feet. Seconds later, he was back by my side.

"What happened?" she pleaded, confused. Clarissa tried to pull her hands in front of her and seemed surprised that she couldn't. "Mr. Salvatore?" she asked timidly. "Oh, no," she whispered. "Why did I do that? I shouldn't have done that. Why would I give everyone probiotics?" The blonde girl turned her head toward the mafia don and stared at him with a questioning expression. "Aren't you a friend of my mom's?"

I almost felt sorry for Clarissa. As Clutterbuck led her away, it was clear that Jeeves's had wiped her mind of most of her own history. She seemed lost and confused.

She was *thoroughly* convinced of her own guilt, however, and she prattled on to the chief about her regret for her actions.

"Thank you," Don Salvatore said to Jeeves as

Clutterbuck led the reject half-witch away. "I appreciate your quick action in protecting our secrets in her mind."

"I *didn't* do that for you," the vampire spat back.

The Don stared at Jeeves for a few moments, and then he nodded. "I acknowledge you for wiping her memory nonetheless. It avoids complications." He frowned. "Well, some complications. Her mother will be...unhappy with the situation. It *was*, however, a test," Don Salvatore said coldly glancing after her one last time. "Clearly, she failed. Her consequences are just."

"Loyalty's a one way street with you, isn't it?" I observed dryly. "You know, it's obvious that you"—I turned to look at Mirabelle Saunders—"and you were both aware that something had happened. And that you *let* it happen. You may not be as guilty as she is, but you're pretty close."

"I didn't know anything!" Mayor Saunders shouted, her eyes betraying the lie.

"You may as well stop your denials, Mirabelle," Don Salvatore said, his eyes cutting toward me. "She's aware of your dishonesty. Possibly before you are." He turned full-face toward me and leaned. "Aren't you, mystic?" He looked pleased with his powers of deduction.

Jeeves tensed again.

"I cut the cord between you and Jeeves right in front of you, and you're acting like you deserve a medal for figuring that out," I told Martin's father. "Yep, I'm the mystic, which means this is *my* town." I narrowed my eyes. "And as the mystic, I think it's time for *you* to go home."

His dark eyes assessed me with interest as he stood, arms folded. After a few moments, Don Salvatore tilted his head. "I don't think you have a clue what powers you hold. If you did, you would have figured this out days ago."

"Are you prepared to gamble on that, Marty?" I bluffed.

Marty Sr. looked so much like Martin. It was a little bit unnerving. As angry as I'd been at Martin, as much as I distrusted him at times, he didn't have the same menace in his face as his father did. Don Salvatore's very stance radiated risk.

"It's true, I arrived here to find out whether the mystic had returned. That old woman was far beyond her prime and no threat to me," he said, his voice just a little harder now. Unbeknownst to him, Miss Bessie stood behind him, swiping at his head and muttering. "And now, I know. So, you are right. It is time for me to go home. I did what I showed up to do."

He stepped back and melded into the half-witch group. Altogether, they turned and walked away—leaving the terrified mayor standing with us and confused about what to do.

"Jeeves," Don Salvatore called over his shoulder without breaking stride. "Are you coming?"

Taking no time to think about it, Jeeves refused.

The last thing Don Salvatore heard was the scream of Mirabelle Saunders as the vampire flew at her to wipe her memory of that which she shouldn't know.

TWENTY-ONE

It took a couple more days to get everyone recovered. Though the antibiotics shot through the city's pipes and out everyone's faucets, Pepper decided she needed to chase after exhausted citizens with a blow dart until the bitter end.

"Some folks don't *like* water," she shrugged while helping to hang Azalea's art on the walls. "So I'm doing them a favor. Quit judging me."

"You just like blowing darts at people," Ollie said.

"You cut up dead people, so between the two of us, which hobby is less gross?" she asked with a toss of her head.

"That's not a hobby, it's my job—"

"Like that's not worse." Turning, she raised her eyebrow. "Have you heard from the vampire?"

"Nope." I finished sweeping and rested the broom against the wall. "I figure he and Martin had a lot to talk about, all things considered. Or maybe the Witch Queen is tying him back up to the mafia boss." I jumped up on the counter and swung my legs. "Or maybe they left town with his father. Who knows."

Pepper shook her head no. "He's still in town. Well, Jeeves is, anyway." Pepper turned slowly and pointed toward Martin's home, Grigio Hills. "I can kinda feel his proximity to me in this weird way. Like I'm a vampire compass."

"You'd be very useful in a horror movie," Gabe said as he walked into the front room with two bags of trash. "I got the back cleaned up. Since your magic whoozy-whatsis kept people out, it wasn't that bad." Gabe tilted his head. "I think a lot of it was from Azalea, actually."

"Why is my son cleaning that woman's store?" I heard Mary ask Miss Bessie snidely. "She has two arms, and she's a witch to boot. Clearly, she can manage on her own."

"Mary Wilcox, you're going to have to get over yourself a little bit," Miss Bessie told her daughter. "Fortuna is a nice young lady—mostly—and your judgment of her is way off base."

Mary glowed an indignant pinkish-red for a moment. "We'll ask the ladies in the two bottles she's left stoppered how they feel about her. I'm sure it will be insightful."

"You know I can hear you, right?" I said as I reached through Mary Wilcox and picked a set of books off a chair she was mimicking sitting on.

She glared at me. "I know you can hear me. Why would I bother saying it otherwise?"

I returned her glare with a steely glance.

"Ignore her," Miss Bessie told me, her insubstantial hand waving in front of my face. "I know you're probably feeling all high and mighty after a nasty look chased Don Salvatore out of town—"

"It was a *little* more than a dirty look, Miss Bessie."

"Okay, a dirty look and a threat," Miss Bessie responded. "But you managed to use the one thing you'd learned just hours before to scare him into shutting up and hightailing it out of here." She gave me a side-eye glance and got up, standing tall to look down at me. "That's a trick that's only going to work once."

"Miss Bessie's yammering about training, isn't she?" Pepper asked.

"I was *about* to if the un-magical humans would button their traps for a minute!" the old woman snapped with a harsh glare at Pepper. "Now, like I said—that's only going to work once. I know you've been focusing on the greyhounds and building your business, but time's up, Delphi. You threw down a gauntlet, but you don't have a sword for the fight."

I stared at the old woman and instinctively prepared to defend myself—but there was no point. I'd realized everything she was saying already. "I know, and you're right—I can't argue with you."

"Now, don't you argue with me!" Miss Bessie told me sternly.

I blinked. "I'm not. You're right. I need to get serious about learning magic."

"Now, look here, young lady. You need to get serious—wait, what?" Miss Bessie stared at me, her mouth open. "Did you just agree with me that you need to get serious?"

"Well, before today, I was the only full witch in town. That meant no one was more powerful—well, magic-wise—than me," I told her. "Even if I didn't know how to use the power, I *had* it, right? And I could study magic crib notes if I needed to in a pinch. Like we did that time at the mansion."

"Not ideal, but go on," Miss Bessie said, nodding.

"I don't know who the Witch Queen is, but I can't believe that she's going to stay out of town now that Don Salvatore knows I'm the mystic." I glanced over at Pepper, who was watching me speak to the ghost. "When she does come back, we need to be ready."

"Maybe they have some information," Mary said, pointing toward the front window.

I turned and saw Jeeves with his fist poised to knock.

Martin stood behind him, looking as glum as I'd ever seen him.

* * *

"Chief Clutterbuck believes everyone has been accounted for and has been given a dose of antibiotics," Martin informed me as he stepped in and moved toward us. "Tourists seemed to stay at the track, at least those that didn't come here to the square to go shopping. Those that tried to leave were caught by the roadblocks."

I nodded. "I actually already know. I talked to Clutterbuck late last night."

"Oh." Martin's face fell. "I'm sorry. I didn't realize that you were still in contact with..." his voice weakly trailed off, and he looked down at the floor. Martin's eyes had dark circles underneath them, and his face was pale. His ordinarily crisp button-down shirt was wrinkled.

He sounded like he'd been through the wringer.

"Martin," Jeeves said sternly. His handsome face slowly turned up, and he looked at his vampire bodyguard. "She doesn't blame you. This wasn't your fault."

Well, *that* was a hop, skip, and a jump farther than *I* would go, but Jeeves turned his head and looked at me sharply before I could say anything. "Martin, where have you been this whole time?" I asked him, ignoring Jeeves's statement so I didn't have to confirm or deny it. "As soon as your father showed up, you disappeared."

Pepper and Ollie continued straightening book displays I knew for a fact were already straight, dusted, and ready for re-opening. Their hair was pulled back over ears trained in our direction. Miss Bessie and Mary sat off to the side, watching. Heck, even Spike and Gideon wandered in from upstairs as if they sensed something was going on they should witness.

"He's my father," Martin said, his voice echoing deeply with pain. "He's my father, you understand? Yes, he's the head of a crime family, and yes, he can be a cruel man, but...but he's my father just the same." He scrutinized my face as if trying to weigh how much to say based on my reaction. Suddenly, Martin shook his head, taking in another deep breath. "But he went too far."

I stepped closer and placed my hand on his arm. "What happened?"

"He arrived unexpectedly." Anger flared on his face. "I think Jerome reported to him that Aunt Addie stopped looking for the bottles. All of a sudden, without explanation. I think that's what started this all. He also reported that you and Miss Bessie had been close before she died."

Jerome was Martin's butler—a dour human that Aunt Addie once told me had been placed there as Don Salvatore's spy. Or maybe it was Jeeves that told me. Anyway, since Aunt Addie was a partial witch and Jeeves was a vampire, they had kept things from Jerome—and Martin's father—pretty easily.

"Why does your father care if there's a mystic in Mystic's End?" I asked.

"Because the mystic is the only one that can release the women from their witch bottle prisons," Jeeves said as Martin shifted like there was a rock in his shoe. "It became clear this past week from what we overheard that Marty Sr. is adamant that Martin's mother never be released."

I almost cracked a smile as Jeeves said *Marty Sr.* so casually. "What do you mean?"

"He threatened me," Martin deadpanned. "And my aunt. And Jeeves." His eyes rose up. "And you.

If we open any of the bottles, he said, we'll
regret it."

"But why? Why does he care so much about
these bottles?"

"I don't know," he answered. "I wish I did. But
to be perfectly honest with you, I don't care."
Martin's face flushed with color, and he got a little
of his tough-guy confidence back. "She's my
mother. I won't leave her—or anyone else—locked
up like that for eternity."

Gideon made a cooing sound in his throat and
pressed against Martin.

"And the whole poisoning the town thing?"
Pepper asked.

"That was just dumb luck," he told her. "My
father's short on cash, and Clarissa chose this
moment to be an idiot." Martin shrugged. "I think
his attention was elsewhere as it happened, and
once it tripled the money coming into the casino, he
decided not to intervene."

I narrowed my eyes at Martin. "Wait a minute.
How can the head of a crime family be short on
cash?"

"I don't know. There's a lot I *do* know, and I'm
willing to tell you whatever you want, so you'll trust
me, Fortuna." Martin stepped forward and placed
his hands on my shoulders. "But there's a lot I don't
know."

Jeeves looked away from Martin and me, his face stony. I waited for the *visus* to show me the silver cord between them, the sign from the universe I should cut that tie, too—but nothing appeared. I wanted to hear Martin's side of the story, but I knew why they were here.

One thing at a time.

Since I didn't know what else to say to Martin, I turned toward the vampire. "And how are you doing since I clipped your chains?" I asked Jeeves.

"You and I should talk about that later. Privately."

"You told Martin, though, didn't you?" I asked openly.

Maybe I should have waited and talked to him about it privately, but again—I knew why they were here. Before I opened those bottles upstairs, I wanted everything out in the open that could be out in the open.

"Martin is aware of what you did, yes," the vampire nodded.

"Are you okay with it?" I asked Martin.

His face twisted with pain, and he didn't answer.

"You did what you had to do," Jeeves told me. "Martin understands that."

I looked curiously at Martin. He didn't *look* like he understood. He didn't feel like it, either—a storm of desperation was surging inside him. He seemed lost. Lost and unsure of what to do.

"All of this can wait," Jeeves said as he squeezed Martin's shoulder. Turning he asked if I was ready to do what needed to be done. Once I said yes, we walked upstairs as if we were marching in a funeral procession.

* * *

"So, I just open it?" I asked Miss Bessie.

"How would I know?" she asked, but her tone was peculiarly gentle. "I wasn't here when you did it the first time. But just pulling out the stopper would seem to be a good place to start, no?"

I pulled.

But it wouldn't come uncorked.

I pushed up on it, and then pulled on the top. Then I tried to wiggle it. Nothing.

"Did my father do something to you? Will this no longer work?" Martin asked, heartbroken.

"Tell handsome over there to calm down," Miss Bessie told Jeeves over her shoulder as she walked up to me. "Now, when you opened Mary's bottle, what were you doing? Exactly?"

"Pepper and I were kind of tussling over it." I closed my eyes and thought back. "I was holding the bottle part, and she pulled the cork.

"Okay, let's do that, then," I said, and explained to Pepper what Miss Bessie had suggested.

She scrambled over and stood in front of me, her hands wrapped around the stopper. "Ready?" she asked, her eyes alight. "One, two, three!" She yanked hard, but the cork stayed put and she flew across the room, crashing into the chair behind her. "What the heck? Was I doing something different?"

"Have her try with the vampire," Mary suggested, her eyes fixed on Jeeves.

"The vampire?" Miss Bessie asked, dubious. "Why him?"

"The reporter's blood was filled with magic. Deadly magic, but still—she was the other side of a magical circuit. Yes, the mystic must be present for the bottles to be opened, but there must be more to it than that," Mary told her mother. "We've had mystics through the ages, and none of you have been able to get a single one of us out until her." Mary pointed. "Perhaps it wasn't *just* her."

"Miss Addie did say something about not being powerful enough." I looked at Jeeves. "We're the only two paranormals here. It might work. If she's right, anyway."

"I'm right, I'm sure of it," Mary said with confidence.

"What?" Pepper asked, her eyes skipping back

and forth between Jeeves and me. "What'd I do wrong?"

Jeeves didn't look quite as confident as Mary, but he walked over. At the same time, I explained to Martin, Pepper, Gabe, and Ollie what Mary hypothesized was the problem. The vampire stood in front of me, his eyes staring intensely into mine. He nodded and reached up as I secured my grip on the bottle.

With a small pop, the cork came out in Jeeves's hand. It took barely any effort, and scarcely any time before the bottle in my hand glowed. The sparkling fog flowed, the lights popped, and the humans in the room gasped as they stared.

"Isn't it pretty?" Pepper breathed, mesmerized.

"Here," I held out the other bottle to Jeeves, and he pulled off the cork. The glittery smoke volume doubled, and the bulbs flickered again while Gideon chased the flashes of light within the clouds on my floor.

"I guess you and I really are stuck with one another," Jeeves whispered as he stepped beside me and watched the cloudy haze pull in and take two forms. He gave me a look I couldn't quite decipher —affection...mixed with some frustration. "Whether we like it or not."

"It's better than being stuck in a bottle for two hundred years," I whispered back as the two women's forms solidified. Their colonial-era gowns were covered by stiff aprons, their hair hidden beneath simple cotton caps. Their expressions were confused.

"Pray pardon me," the one on the right in blue said to Martin, directly next to her. "Where is this place? And who are you?" She looked around the room. "Is this Mystic? Have we been freed?"

"You have," I said, nodding. I gave the woman a warm smile. "I know this must be incredibly traumatic for you, but please know that no one will hurt you."

"Sisters," Mary said, rushing to embrace the women in her arms. "What flowers were you?"

"You must be the rose!" the woman in red told Mary excitedly. "I am the lavender!"

"And I am just the dandelion," the woman in blue said, bowing her head delicately.

"Well, I'm confused," I murmured.

"Is it her?" Martin asked, his eyes filled with tears. "Is one of them my mother?"

As the ghosts gathered in a corner talking excitedly and I explained to Gabe, Ollie, and Pepper what we were seeing, Jeeves comforted a heartbroken Martin.

TWENTY-TWO

"Well," Miss Bessie said as she settled down next to me and leaned in. "We have new information." The older ghost glanced at her daughter—who was huddled in a corner with the two colonial women—and bent in even further, her voice dropping to a whisper. "Knowledge we *could* have had the moment we uncorked Mary, but apparently she didn't feel it was important to share."

Pepper and I looked at each other. "What new information?"

"Each one of the witch bottles has a particular flower in them," Miss Bessie said, pointing. "Her bottle had rose, that one lavender, that one dandelion. Over time, they learned to use their flower's connection to other flowers to travel out of...out of..." Miss Bessie clearly wanted to say out-of-body. Still, since the women had no bodies, the phrase wasn't entirely accurate. "Anyway, it's how they were capable of moving about a little."

"That's how they knew each other's flower—they were able to communicate with one another that way," Pepper guessed in response to Miss Bessie's statement. "I'd read somewhere that plants talk to each other through their roots underground, but this is just wild. But that they could communicate with each other through their flowers? That's crazy."

Miss Bessie frowned. "Well, if their plants grew nearby, they could. And I should point out it's no wilder than you being able to sense the vampire's direction simply because he bit you."

The five of us—Miss Bessie, Pepper, Gabe, Ollie, and I—turned to look at Jeeves and Martin in another corner talking. Well, Pepper and I turned first. Gabe and Ollie turned without having a clue what Miss Bessie just said or why we were looking.

Pepper thought about it and nodded in the old woman's direction. "Good point."

Wait a minute...how did she look in Miss Bessie's direction?

"Do you have your *Ghosts, Ghosts* app on?" I asked Pepper.

"No, why?"

"Because you're *talking* to Miss Bessie," I replied, pointing at the ghost. "Can you see her?"

Pepper turned and laughed. "Yeah, I guess I can. Huh. How about that." Pepper looked the old woman up and down. "You look pretty good for an ancient, dead grandma."

"And you're as respectful as ever, child," Miss Bessie responded wryly. "When did this start?"

"When the corks popped and all that smoke was swirling around?" Pepper said, waving her arms. "It just sort of all came into focus. Like, everyone just appeared out of the smoke." She sat back in her chair and smiled. "I gotta tell you, I'm super digging this *Pepper gets superpowers* byproduct of whatever we're doing."

"Jeeves can see you," I told Miss Bessie. "Maybe it's a side effect of her vampire bite."

Ollie, who had been silently following the conversation, turned a little green as he stared at his girlfriend's excited face. He swallowed and then sighed. "You're never going to give this up, are you?"

Pepper smiled even wider and punched him in the shoulder. "Why would I? Would *you*?"

I waved a hand at the two in hopes I could avert the argument I knew was coming. "How old are they?" I asked Miss Bessie, pointing toward the two ghosts.

"Hundreds of years old," she answered, frowning again. "In fact, it seems they were contained when this town was still called Mystic. Which makes no sense at all."

"Why not?" Pepper asked, ignoring Ollie's defeated stare.

"Because history says the town changed when the guys showed up," Miss Bessie said. The old woman shifted uncomfortably, and worry lines appeared on her face. "They knew nothing of the men that appeared or the town changing. They only remember a town of women. Their coven. And their capture."

"That can't be right. If it is, that would mean..." I trailed off.

Miss Bessie nodded. "Exactly. One of their coven sisters knew. The history we have? It's wrong. Or worse—"

"One of the women in Mystic, in the coven, betrayed them," Pepper said, her face sad.

* * *

"So, how is he?" I asked Jeeves as we sat on the curb behind my shop. The vampire and I had slipped out the back to talk privately, away from the rest of the group.

"Martin? He's having a difficult time with all the things that have come to pass." The vampire sat next to me on the curb, staring down at the asphalt. The sun had set, it was dark, and the moon showed brightly over the town. It bathed us in an unearthly glow. After days of chaos, Mystic's End was quiet. "He's a strong man. He'll figure out how to process his father's betrayal and guilt, and he'll stand tall once more." Jeeves cut his eyes to me and half-smiled. "It may take a few days."

"Why do you have such intense loyalty to him?" Jeeves's face showed no surprise at my question. "This kind of care, that's not something that can be forced by a magical tie. At least not that I've ever heard about or seen."

"I told you that I entered into this willingly." Jeeves leaned back, resting his weight on his hands and kicking his feet out in front of him. "And I did. I got what I wanted for what I've given, and it was something I never could have got on my own."

I nodded. "So, you've said. But what is that? What did you get from these people that made an eternity like this worth it?"

"A life," he whispered. He gazed up at the moon and closed his eyes as if trying to absorb the energy he would need to speak about what he promised me he would. After a few moments, he cleared his throat. "More specifically, my sister's."

"You have a sister?"

"In another existence," he smiled wistfully. "Christina. My twin."

"Christopher and Christina," I said, remembering his original name. "Martin told me a little bit about you, but not that. I had no idea."

"How could you?" he asked. "Our tie has been severed by my death. There's nobody to sense, even for you, because there is nothing there. All that is replaced by the blood connection when someone decides—or is forced—to experience this form of death."

I could sense nothing from him, but I could read the pain on his face. I wanted to ask dozens of questions—how could he have left his own sister, a twin no less? How did she react when he left, when he broke the tie between them? Did he ever see her, talk to her, or did she think him genuinely dead?

But I asked nothing. I let him tell his tale.

"When we were born, we were...different. I was born healthy. So healthy that I was an athlete, an outdoorsman. As a child, I took that health for granted. Eventually, I understood—my sister was delivered with a heart defect," he told me as if reciting a rehearsed speech. "She was sickly, weak. She endured so many surgeries and suffered so many ills that I had to stop trying to comprehend them. The doctors warned us next year, she would likely die—every year they said the same thing," he laughed bitterly. "Next year it would be over. Prepare for it." The vampire caught my eyes and grinned proudly. "The doctors didn't know Christina. My sister? She defied them all."

I smiled, gently blinking back tears. "She sounds like a remarkable person."

"She is," Jeeves nodded. The smile slowly faded, overtaken by gloom. "And I...was not. I got in trouble at school, ran with a tough crowd. I put my poor mother through a hell that she didn't deserve considering most of her time and attention, and energy went toward just keeping Christina alive. I was a greedy child," he said sadly, his face falling. "I was jealous of the concern she got. I didn't understand the anguish I was causing, the stress I was adding to."

"Well, you were an adolescent, Jeeves—"

"No," he answered sharply. "Do *not* let me out of my responsibility for the pain I caused. Do not excuse it or minimize it. I made life harder for everyone." He paused, his face twisting with grief. "And then I destroyed it. I wrecked my car after a night of drinking, and my father came to get me." Jeeves looked down, blood welling up in his eyes. "He never arrived. In an utter twist of irony, his vehicle was plowed into by a drunk driver running a stop sign. He was killed." His head was so low that his chin nearly brushed his chest. "The drunk driver had been at the same party I was. I knew him. I could have *been* him."

"Oh, Jeeves," I whispered. "I'm so sorry." I reached out and gently caressed his shoulder, but he shrugged it away.

"I deserve no consolation. None. My father does. My mother does. My sister does." He breathed deeply and then exhaled harshly. "But, I do not."

I opened my mouth to argue with him, to say everyone deserved sympathy for their pain, that he was young and people make mistakes—sometimes mistakes with horrible consequences. That he couldn't punish himself for that endlessly.

And then I realized that was *precisely* why he was what he was.

He wanted to punish himself.

Forever.

"I tried to make up for my mistakes. I joined the military to help protect my mother and sister, but it wasn't enough. Medical insurance, medical bills...I was ill-adapted to support a family. Nothing in my irresponsible youth had readied me for it. And then I heard whispers in my unit. Soldiers said the uptick in deaths were *not* deaths at all—men were leaving, going AWOL. They all wanted to join some private security firm that was paying thousands, millions, even, to produce super-soldiers. I had to know if the rumors were true."

"You wanted the money for your family."

Jeeves dipped his head briefly. "But when I finally tracked them down, they offered me far more than that," he said, turning. "Marty Sr. knew all about me before I even opened my mouth at the interview. About my sister, my mother. He was looking for someone to be a personal guard to his son. If I would agree to be obliged to him, bound to *them*, and to never leave? In exchange for that, not only would he give my family more money than they could ever need..." Jeeves took a deep breath. "He swore to heal my twin. Completely."

I hadn't met this Witch Queen yet, but my stomach churned with nausea at the idea that any witch could use something like this as leverage, as a bargaining chip for a life of servitude. It was disgusting. Witches I knew with healing powers healed because it was *right*. Not as payment in some underworld scheme. I swallowed the churning urge to punch her in the face.

Whoever she was.

"To make a long story short, I took the deal," he said, smiling. "My mother and sister aren't rich— that promise was a bit overblown—but they were given enough to stabilize their lives. My sister had a miraculous recuperation. The doctors are still arguing over how she could have spontaneously recovered from something they were sure would kill her. The defect was structural—spontaneous healing simply doesn't happen with what she has."

"Do they know what you did?" I asked.

"My mother and sister? No." He peered down again, his voice lowering. "They think I was killed in a secret operation in Afghanistan, and the money they received was life insurance."

We sat quietly. I stared at Jeeves's face, my eyes searching for his. For a moment, he looked up, and we locked each other in a stare so intense I felt the weight of it. His eyes were soft as they gazed into mine. But still guarded. Still hiding something. "There's more, isn't there?"

"There's always more, Fortuna." Jeeves turned toward me, his expression strained. "But I'm sharing this with you for two reasons. One is that you asked me to so you could trust me. I don't know whether this goes to that or not, but the second reason is the one more important to me."

"Okay," I said hesitantly.

"The magic that ties me to Martin can kick off consequences should it snap. There were no consequences for me—other than the obvious discomfort you witnessed—when the connection between Marty Sr. and me snapped." His back was ramrod straight, his tone suddenly sporting an uncomfortable edge. "That is *not* the case for my link with Martin. I know that you can damage those connections, but I am *begging* you to leave the one between Martin and me alone."

I tilted my head. "What happens if I don't?" I took care to make my voice soft, so what I said couldn't be misinterpreted as a threat. The last thing I wanted to do was bring the tortured vampire soldier even more worry. And to be honest? I knew the answer to the question before I ever asked it.

But I had to ask it.

"My sister becomes ill again. Her suffering comes back. Her misery, her agony." His eyes were intense, his voice twisted with anguish at the idea of it. "She is *happy* now, Fortuna, because of what I did. She's going to college, she has a boyfriend. Christina is slowly building the life she *should* have had. Even with my loss, the loss of our father, her resilience has seen her through." Jeeves told me proudly though he looked at me with anxious trepidation. "I've given up too much to give her and my mother this, to perform penance for my mistakes. I beg you not to punish her this way. Please."

I don't know what story I imagined he would tell me, but this wasn't it. Jeeves was so cold when I first met him, almost an automaton of a man. He had always seemed uncaring, aloof. The past few months, I wondered if there was something beneath that distant, icy demeanor. Something more to him than the criminal killing machine he appeared designed to be.

"This is why, even if Martin's wrong, you have to be loyal to him," I whispered.

Jeeves gritted his teeth. Then he nodded.

"I'm so sorry this has happened to you," I told him wearily, unsure of how to comfort a man so beaten down by trauma inflicted from without and within. "The story is tragic from its beginning to the present day, and I hope the ultimate ending is happier than what we have now." I wavered continuing—this was obviously torture for Jeeves—but after a few seconds, I pushed forward with more questions. "Can I ask you something?"

"Of course."

"Is it just the tie that binds you to Martin? You *seem* to really care about him." I hesitated again. "Is that just a show?"

"No," he smiled. "Remember when I told you Martin was working to change his father's family? That he was trying to stop the horrible things his father does?" I nodded. "If Martin succeeds, my family will be safe and no one will make my sister suffer again. That's a brave—and dangerous—thing to attempt. I respect him for seeing the wrong in it all and struggling to correct it."

The rear door swung open, and Pepper stuck her head out. "Are you two done yet? We're hungry."

"So eat," I called across the alley. "We'll be back in. Just give us a minute."

"First, you have no food in your house, and Gabe's tiny hot dogs in pastry aren't going to do it. We want to go to the diner. You've had an hour, Delphi," Pepper said, tapping her wrist as she leaned against the heavy metal door. "Time's running out."

Time's running out. Her words hung in the air.

I stood up and reached down to help Jeeves to his feet. We stood close to one another, hands still linked, eyes locked. I felt the surge of attraction flutter in my stomach as we stared, and I again tried to push it out of my awareness.

Vampire dazzle. That's all it was—vampire dazzle.

"Thank you for trusting me with your story," I told him sincerely.

He bowed his head in a quick nod. "Thank you for protecting my sister."

I blinked. "You know, I never actually said I *wouldn't* break the tie."

"I realize you didn't." The vampire gazed at me

affectionately. "But you won't. You won't hurt her or put her at risk. Of that, I have no doubt."

With all that had happened, everything that had been spoken, it felt wrong to smile at him.

But I did.

He smiled back.

I didn't know why he counted on me, but it was clear that he did. Trusted me with the most precious thing in the world to him. Gazing into his eyes, I promised myself I would take away the knife that hung over his sister's head, threatening her destruction for his disloyalty.

Somehow.

Miss Bessie was right.

It was time to get to work.

THANK YOU FOR READING!
I hope you enjoyed Boozehounds and Ball Drops! Please think about leaving a review! Fortuna and Gideon's adventures continue in Book 7, Scry Harder!

KEEP UP WITH LEANNE LEEDS

Thanks so much for reading! I hope you liked it! Want to keep up with me?

Visit leanneleeds.com to:

Find all my books...

Sign up for my newsletter...

Like me on Facebook...

Follow me on Twitter...

Follow me on Instagram...

Thanks again for reading!

Leanne Leeds

FIND A TYPO? LET US KNOW!

Typos happen. It's sad, but true.

Though we go over the manuscript multiple times, have editors, have beta readers, and advance readers it's inevitable that determined typos and mistakes sometimes find their way into a published book.

Did you find one? If you did, think about reporting it on leanneleeds.com so we can get it corrected.